D0095186

HOMEPLACE

HOMEPLACE

MARISTAN CHAPMAN

author of

"The Happy Mountain"

GROSSET & DUNLAP

by arrangement with

VIKING ~ PRESS

PRINTED IN U. S. A.

To

FRANCIS LYNDE

Many are beholden for shelter, and the comfort of quiet words, yet come they crave to journey on he leaves them travel.

HOMEPLACE

CHAPTER I

THE last quiet breath of night was spent and light was just being made, when Bess Howard came to the front door of the house and looked abroad. She shut the door softly, and sat herself down upon the edge of the porch, her mind yet quivering with the uneasiness of sleep that had run away too soon. A dark green wrapper was pulled close around her slight-made body, and her uncombed yellow hair flared above her puzzled eyes, so that she looked more like a chrysanthemum flower than not.

She waited for day to happen.

On the far edges the circling woods about the farmstead were slate-colored, for the heavy-footed time of year was come, and a spicy smell of late fall was crushed from the fields and forest trees around Glen Hazard. Each morning the careful sun crept up and took ever a shorter way across the sky, and the year plodded on, dragging unwilling days athwart the world and thrusting them one by one out of sight behind the hills westerly.

Up to these days life was only pictures of things to Bess Howard. When she looked at the passing time, she found the earth good or, when a thing failed to pleasure her, she turned to look elsewhere—willful as a new robin, and no more to blame. And now, here was life waiting to be spoken to, and Bess with no words ready.

She walked as far as the gate and looked back on the homeplace that slept in the shelter of the orchard, close in the shadow of the many-branched dooryard maple. There sat the old log house, the same that she had been born in. The logs were weatherworn and sunken, and the stone chimney sloped over one end as commonly as an old habit. And within doors were just her sister and the crippled father.

Bess tried to think about the house looking like this on her borning day; and the time, only a few years after, when her mother had been carried away, and Bess herself had sat in a flower-border watching the many people come and go above her. She recalled trying to catch their shadows as they drifted by, but always they got away. And she wondered if she was yet trying to catch shadows. That long-ago night, when she cried for her mother-woman, there came only Dena to her, saying: "Hush you and sleep, Honey." And she had crept in beside her—and Dena not more than eight years old her ownself!

Then there was the day her father had been brought home, after falling off a roof he'd been carpentering, and sat always in his chair thereafter, ordering life as best he could, while Dena grew up to take all care on herself. And just this short while back there was Dena getting wed. That was a cheerfuller thing, but the house made no matter between borning, and wedding, and dying.

"A homeplace is like that," Bess told herself. "Hit wraps a person around; hit's where things happen to a person."

This morning the house was close-shuttered and had the same stubbornness her father owned. It sat there as if nothing could move it forever, and he, withindoors, complained a sight in the world did any new thing take place, such as Dena's being wed, or herself about to take Fayre Jones, or the roadmen wanting a through-way over the properties. Bess could see the torn earth of the new road cut coming over from Glen Hazard, licking its way toward them. And the homestead stood squarely across its way.

In all the world was only the least underbreath of living, and the quiet waiting of birds before their day's business should begin. The solid stillness pushed at the earth and rolled it toward the sun.

Bess began to feel shivery, and came aware that she was not yet dressed, so she went in, and Dena, building a fire in the kitchen stove, asked, "Where in sense you been to a'ready?"

Bess answered: "You all time shaking at me to be early up, and gin I do get out o' bed you only bite a person."

While she dressed, she kept on making pictures in her head, and directly the house was full of the smell of coffee and fresh-baked bread. Dena called her to help set breakfast forward, and Bess with yet only one shoe on.

"Hit's only I was studying on matters," she excused herself, and Dena said: "Time enough to go cloud-walking when dishes is set aside."

She helped her father into his chair and dragged him up to the breakfast table, and he fretted that she was unhandy at it.

"As well get used to you first as last," he said, "since Dena'll be gone away directly."

Homer Howard took life peacefully most days,

but this morning he was, like Bess, all in a twitchet, and would touch no food but his glass of milk. So Bess pulled him to the forward-room fire, and packed him up with his piece-quilt around him and his useless feet on a cracker-box, but she saw that his eyes followed Dena, who was smoothing up the beds, shaking out curtains, and setting all things upright. At last Dena took up a basket of sewing work and sat down by the firehearth over against Homer. Then he was content and all the day was before him.

Bess could see them from the kitchen where she washed the dishes. Homer's tousled hair and bright eyes were lively in a shadowed corner, but a streak of sun was glancing on Dena's smooth dark hair and gentle face. Bess put down a saucer and stood twirling the dish towel.

"Hit'll be plumb funny, gin Dena's gone," she said to herself. "Looks like I never did content him the way she does. He 'n' me'll likely quarrel days long. And all the dishes in the world to wash, moreover." She went on slowly, stopping at every cup and plate, and hearing the others talking.

"Soon's I'm gone," Dena began—all Dena's words these times started that way—"soon's I'm gone, you'll not neglect about your wool clothes come cold days."

Homer fretted: "Where's the sense in you going off? What garred you wed with Waits Lowe?"

Dena said: "You seen it coming long enough, and never said you'd care."

" 'Twas the unneighborlest thing Rashe and Barsha done me. They and us living next neighbors these long years and they got no more kindness than to leave their boy come robbing me of my usefullest girl. 'Tis plain thieving."

"You're knowen of Rashe Lowe," Dena said mildly. "Leave Waits get a craving, and Rashe thinks himself President and right away orders it done."

Bess now came in from the kitchen place and perched on the arm of Homer's chair.

"I declare," she said to Dena, " 'twill be a mercy when you're gone off, the way we're all on edge about every day'll be the last. You're neither here nor ain't."

Dena tossed her a sleeve to baste up and said: "There's scant stuff to finish with, and white thread's about gone."

"Which spells I take me down to the store again.

Person'd think you was wed to a city man—all these clothes! This blue silk is pretty stuff to the feel."

"Hit's the piece Aunt Matt give me," Dena said. "Sam and Aunt Matt's the givingest people in these-abouts, in spite of they're all time talking about getting rich. Look at the way they cherish Morris Ott since a accident overtook him, and no other-where for him to go. Which recalls, you'd as well happen by their place, efn time holds out, and make thanks for this goods."

They were fere together in the brightening morning, while the old man looked out of the window, and the girls sewed on Dena's new clothes. The low room was quiet, but there was a restlessness where content used commonly.

"There's ne'er a thing like a tree for taking the edge offen time," Homer said directly. "That door-yard tree now. I gather back in mind to the time it was scarce more'n a walking-stick. And orchard trees —mostly every one I hand-raised my ownself."

"Which way out is this sleeve due to turn?" Bess asked, and Dena handed her the other to match it with.

Homer went on: "Seems these crack-eyed road-makers got no feelings for a man's trees, the way they come around offering cash money. My homeplace nor trees ain't for sale, I tell 'em."

"They'll claim they're bound to get a throughway," Bess said.

"They'd as good take it around Robbins' Gap." Homer's dark eyes snapped, and he said again, "Money for my trees! Hit ain't reason. Commonplace money for what's took me all my days to grow 'n' tend."

Bess and Dena went on sewing, while Homer jerked and muttered and shook a thin fist at the road workings that showed all wobbledy through his window glass.

Directly came a chick-a-dee's cry to warm their ears, and Homer said: "Take for a sample! What'd *he* do gin I leave 'em cut through the orchard place? Likely them fool roadmakers might give him dollar-bills to make a nest of."

The bird said: "—v—ptt—!" And he fussed and chattered in the dooryard tree, while Homer went on perfectly like him withindoors, until the morning carried off their quarreling.

Bess stood up and stretched, and went to the front door to waste time as the longest way of getting back kitchen to start dinner. She perked her head on one side and listened.

"There comes that worthless chase-world that you're wed to," she called to her sister. "I hear his fiddle. Hit sounds like the wind getting up."

Dena gave over the careful folding of sewing things and tossed all in a heap into the basket and was gone.

Bess came in and stood before Homer, and he was looking out of the window, where Waitstill and Dena were together. At last his eyes came around to hers, and she said on a sudden:

"Time Dena gets gone sure enough . . ."

"Oh, for track's sake!" Homer shouted.

". . . d'you reckon me and you'll fuss *all* the time?"

Homer said gloomily: "Most likely."

And Bess went out kitchen.

CHAPTER II

It was the useless hour of three o'clock, and the day was used up and full of old smells that drifted through the dusty sunlight of the September afternoon. Gleaming white thunderheads crept up back of the hills and stared down at Glen Hazard where it lay fretful and fevered in the hollow. The lower houses, with doors flung wide, were choking for air; and the topmost shacks upon the slopes looked as though they had scrambled up so far and then given over for very hotness.

Down in town's center, horses stood unhitched with drooping heads, and dogs lay sleeping like dead things in streaks of thin shadow. Black dust hung over the cinder streets, pitch boiled from the stacked tie-timber along the flashing railroad tracks; and the gauge on the water tank showed only three feet.

Where Ranson Gillow's General Store was huddled at the knot of the crossroads, citizens shifted in and out and fell to snapping over nothing. Idle and restless at the same time, none could find a place to go save in another's way. Some going into the store out of the sun, and others pushing out seeking air—and there being only one door—they got more inflamed each passing minute.

Among the townsmen stirred the roadmakers, newly come in from their camp above Big Gully Hill, and they found all in Glen Hazard unfriendly, for the new road was a hateful thing. There was yet no open cause for quarrel, but all were craving a happening to take place, so they could be after it.

In back of the store Bess Howard hurried her trading, for the stranger men were bold to speak and she had no liking for their roughness. It was no surprise the men would plague her to talk, for Bess had gold, shining hair, and dark blue eyes that were apt for fun and quick to tears and held a mischief that was kin to both. Furthermore, her mouth was shapely and her nose just a dot to finish off with.

She went out of the store and beyond Glen Hazard homewards with a free step. It was no easy going up Cragg Hill in the thick of the heat with a double-end sack all knobbledy with packages, bumping and beating against her. But she struggled on to a patch of shade by a boulder near the crest, and threw down her burden and sat herself on top of it. Here she might handily count what money she had left, and when it was not as much as she wished, she turned it over to see if it would add up to more on the other side.

"Gin a person buys their needs," she said, "there's not enough left over to salt a batch o' bread."

She heard the tread of a horse climbing the hill, and the flung rocks from its hooves go trickling down the roadway. Directly Preacher Virgil Howard, on his gant white horse, rode up into a streak of melted sunshine, with his eyes screwed up tight against the brightness. He was a welcome old man to all young things, and Bess smiled to see him now, for his nose and beard were standing forth in stern warning, as if he made up a sermon. Almost they rode over Bess where she sat by the roadside.

"Amen!" he cried out, when his horse swung outwards; and he opened his eyes to take part in worldly affairs again.

"What you doing only so far along, Bess? You left town ever ago."

"This store stuff hefted more than I counted on," she said. "A fine trail you're making for the automobiles, the way you leave your horse scutter rocks."

"They'll not much use along this way, gin the wide open road gets graded," he answered easily, while he got down. "Get you up here the while I brogue alongside. You and me'll be at your place right now."

He lifted her up on the horse, which was no great matter even for his old arms, since Bess was built to blow away in a light wind. Then he flung the sack across back of the saddle.

"You aim to buy Ranson Gillow out of stock, or is it a hotel you keep these days?"

Bess said: "Mostly stuff for Dena. Hit's a surprise a person can't get wed without craving to buy a piece of everything on earth. First it was clothes, and now it's kitchen fixments and cloth for towels and sheets, and mercy knows what all."

"Seems she might anyway do her own toting," the Preacher said.

"Former times, she would; more especially since she claims I fling coins away, not judging sorry stuff from good; but Homer's that bereft at her going that he claims to have her around his neck the day long. Always he favored Dena above me, and he can't scarcely abide to have her out of his sight."

Bess pulled up the horse suddenly. "Hear the goings-on?" she asked, while she screwed around in the saddle; and Virgil turned and peered back toward town, and the horse stood with its ears limp—one pointing back and the other forward.

Shouts came up to them and a sound of running feet, as if the town had caught fire at last. Thuds, halloos and the noise of riot filled the air, and the town dogs awoke so their barking came muffled through the heat haze.

"Some person must have stepped on another's toe," Virgil said. "I been looking for a taking-place since noon."

"More 'n likely one o' they roadmakers spoke out of manners."

They listened, while the noise broke out again, and the dogs took spasms of yiping where they got caught under foot. Directly all was quieted.

"I'd not be surprised didn't the Glen Hazard men rid the town of such trash," Virgil said. "In all my years o' memory roadmaking spelled trouble."

They went on over the top of Cragg Hill until the hush of the woods closed around them, for the hills bore great clouds on their shoulders and a weight was on all the world.

"You'll be getting wed yourself in a whip's crack," Virgil went on from where they had left talking.

"Not likely. Homer's bad enough with only Dena's taking off, and gin I talk about me doing so, he gets altogether up his own sleeve. He's that misput owing to the road about to split our place in two that I scarcely got the heart to freck him."

"Still 'n' all, you aim to wed with Fayre Jones."

"Maybe so; maybe not. 'Pends does he get him a homeplace."

Virgil took off his hat the better to cool his head, and his white hair shone in the westering sun. He said: "We had enough back-and-forth over Dena and Waits. For peace's sake I trust you and Fayre will match and settle without ado."

"I'm all tired out with my ownself," Bess owned. "And with Fayre, too. There don't seem much to him, someway. My life's got to be a thing of jagged edges." She was talking to herself more than to the Preacher, but he answered her.

"Pity us, efn you're going the way of Waitstill Lowe. We had our fill of torn-up-ness with him."

"A woman-person fails of going unbounden."

"A man maybe runs the earth such times, but a woman, gin she's garred stay in one place, might maybe paw up the earth around her right smart!"

Where the low road takes off around Red Hill

northerly, Bess stopped the horse and said: "I got to go by Aunt Matt and carry Dena's thanks for her gift."

"What would be the meaning of this foolishment, and the day so late along?"

Bess laughed down at the old man. "Since I got me a horse, seems a pity to waste him."

"And what goes with my old feet?" Preacher complained. "Still 'n' all, I can make it in my way to see Sam Ewart about that lap-siding he promised me ever ago."

Bess picked up the bridle rein and set forward. And they came in right time to Sam Ewart's latest homeplace, and Bess drew up at the gate while Virgil cried the house. Since Sam and Aunt Matt owned a habit of moving house every hand's while, it would have been no surprise to find this place barren and themselves gone, even carrying Morris Ott and his broken leg with them. But now they saw Aunt Matt taking out from the back of the house to the pump, as if the place was afire and she alone to quench it. When she heard the Preacher's voice, she came scurrying across the yard, the empty bucket clacking in her hand.

"Alight and set!" she cried out. "Hit's been a

everlasting spell you've kept away from here."

"So far as lighting down goes, I'm best atop of this beast," Bess told her. "He being so high I'd be disabled to get me up again."

"You're bound to come in and greet Morris Ott," Aunt Matt said. "He's plain starved for talk these days. Virge Howard, you're most liable to find Sam sitting yonder of the mill, unless here he comes now."

Bess slid down from the horse and made thanks for Dena about the piece of silk goods, and then went withindoors to where Morris Ott was bedfast. And she was gentle with him, the way she could be when kindness was topmost in her tumbled head.

"Ain't that leg well yet?" she asked, while she pulled up a chair and sat herself down for talk.

"Not near so well as before I knapped it in two tending Micajah Dobbs' affairs for him," Morris Ott said. "Yet it's better 'n when it was worse."

"Tell how come it," Bess asked. "Hit'll be a sharp time gin the others get over speaking together."

There was not much to be seen of Morris Ott, the way he lay in a dark corner like a wrapped-up log of wood, but even so his face showed him a busy-looking man, with a snub nose in a smooth young face, and bright eyes that shifted eagerly over Bess and welcomed her. Morris Ott was a usual man full of awareness.

"Wasn't nothing only Micajah's old tricks," he said. "Like common when come a happening, Micajah took off so he'd be safe out o' sight, and garred me and Dite Morgan cover the still. Hit was fired up so it was uneasy work, and it took time. We'd no more'n got it scattered than here come the officers. Dite took off up the hill, and me downwards, being in such haste that I mistook the trail and rolled offen a rockledge, and there I was till a man come snooping that late night and found my whereats. He garred Sam loan him the tackle to hoist me up and they got me to Sam's wagon that stood a long piece beyond and fetched me here."

When Bess had turned this over in her mind, she said: "That's a history. Only you'd as well own 'twas Fayre Jones come across you and holp you out."

Morris turned sulky. "I'd as lief not be beholden to him, only I was disabled not. Thought it was me you craved news of."

"Supposing it might be," Bess said. "I'd anyways give thanks where it was due."

"Fayre Jones makes no matter."

"Me being safe pledged to him, you got poor manners."

"Happen you think him 'safe,'" Morris said, after long enough time. "Likely you fail of being knowen how he was scattered from the cradle, same as I was. Both of us took names from the neighbors that cherished us, him from the Joneses and me from the Otts."

"That's common," Bess owned. "Hit don't make a man worse."

"Surely not—me nor Fayre either. All I 'ware you is, efn I was about to wed with Fayre Jones, and it passes me why you crave it, I'd ask his true name. Make him tell how come he's got no forefathers nor family. Happen he fails of it, he'd be a choice one to wed. What tale might you tell your young-uns?"

"Then what of your ownself?" Bess asked sharply.

"That's my affairs. And gin you'd join with me, I'd be glib to tell all. I've anyways got properties."

"Have done with your scawting, you've no such."

"Have so. Bottom-land properties, down Grassy Cove. Fayre don't own more than the clothes he stands in and his wages at the big mill."

Bess had more to think about than had troubled

her yet; but Morris would give no further word.

From the porch came a sprattle of talk, and these two, in a temper together, kept quiet and listened to some others having a difference.

"A preacher like you claim to be," Sam said, "had ought to know other than to blame the Lord's doings on me. Who was it failed of sending rain enough to get the planks sawed out?"

"All is," the Preacher warned him, "you give me harsh promise to put that wood up at my house a month gone, and there's ne'er a splinter in sight."

"Efn you look for it long enough, it'll be there," Sam told him. "What's the fret, Matt, that you go hopping from foot to foot?"

"Ever you get through speaking, I aim to bid these to supper, and coffee ought to be on stove this minute."

"And welcome," Sam said. "Go tend house, Matt."

"Kind thanks," Preacher answered, "and I dislike to deny a welcome, but I'm bound to deliver that trivvet yonder to her homeplace." He lifted up his voice and cried: "We'd best be inching on, Bess."

Now Bess had failed of getting any more news out of Morris Ott, and was content to sit by him to eternity until she learned the meaning about the dark sayings on Fayre Jones.

"I aim to stay on," she called. "You cry in home and tell 'em I'll be along directly."

" 'Tain't fitten I should leave you run loose through the darkling woods," Preacher told her. "Get you up on this horse right now."

"Disabled to," Bess made pert answer, not moving from where she sat. "He's too high."

"Well, pity Fayre Jones, efn this is what he aims to wed. Get you on this horse!"

Bess could judge that it was time to do as the Preacher said; more especially as thunder was growling on the world's edge, so she gave a good-night to Morris, and came out. And being lifted up, she called to Aunt Matt: "Come over to our place soon —you and Sam! Me and Homer'll be lonely gin Dena's away."

As they went along the road, Preacher Howard said: "You're a scandal, you are! Claiming to go talk with Aunt Matt, and scarcely swapped greeting than you took up with Morris Ott."

"Morris tells where Fayre Jones has not got a rightful name, leave alone a homeplace," Bess said.

"And leave me get my ears wore out by Aunt

Matt and Sam," Virgil Howard went on. "Never you pay heed to Morris. Fayre Jones looks to be mild, but he's an unfailing one and of good report, besides being a helpsome boy."

Bess had a headful of strange notions, and directly she said again: "I'm all tired out with my ownself."

"No use to gainstrive," Preacher told her.

They came in sight of the new road workings, at the cut below Big Gully Hill, and the machinery was very close on Howard's Place. The steam shovel stood black against the western sky, and it held its iron head high on its ugly jointed neck.

"I heard tales of such great beasts as that walking the earth in former days," Virgil said, while he gentled the horse that was prancing sideways.

"That scoop thing is walking down on us as sure as if it lived," Bess said. "See it rear back!"

And when they came to the gate of her homeplace, the Preacher lifted Bess down and himself got upon the horse.

"I thank you nicely," Bess said.

"Freely welcome," he told her. "A restful night to you."

Bess took up her sack of store goods, and watched

the old man ride into the night. Thunder yet rumbled back of the woods, and darkness overflowing the valley drowned the heavy hills and washed against the stars.

CHAPTER III

THE sun lifted slowly from behind the hills and burned a path for himself between the great white clouds that boiled and steamed in the storm-brewing sky. Bess Howard found herself worse off than ever when she got up from a troubled night and saw the house in a clutter with Dena's things, and all matters run to seed. She suspected this of being a wastrel day, when household things take a meanness of their own. A day when you put down the paring knife for a minute and it is lost forever.

Bess went to and fro at her sister's call, carrying things, putting them down in one place, and picking them up the next second to make space for others; and some she spread on the porch to get sun in them before they should be packed away. She felt like something that did not matter, being nothing but a fetch-and-carry, and this discontented her. She dodged around Homer, who sat huddled in his chair, a perfect model of misery.

"Leave stumbling on me," he said. "Does seem

like a man peaceful as me ought to be let live without I got to be turned end for end with other folks' bearm."

Meantime, Dena sat solemnly in front of her packing, with her mind already following Wait-Still-on-the-Lord Lowe. She laid shoes above hats and heavy sheeting on top, and had to take all out and do over. Then she forgot what she started to do, and left Bess standing with her arms full of things up to her chin, while she picked up a book and wrote on the front page, *Mrs. W. Lowe, Glen Hazard.* It was no surprise that Bess was altogether misput and out of patience.

And then, with breakfast things yet unwashed, and all in house fit to shame a person before sudden guests, came Waits himself shouting that his house was ready, and where was Dena. She went out to quieten him, and they walked away into the sunlight, leaving Bess to clear up as best might be.

Homer said: "Quit hustling them clothes, you'll get 'em all spoiled. There's no sense raising a dust."

"A person's got to have a place to step," she answered him. "Gin a person's wed, she ought to hasten to her proper home."

And Dena came back into the house and said: "Waits is gone off."

"You've no call to look lost; he'll be back quick enough; he ain't nothing but back these times. Hit's a surprise you failed of bidding him stay eat dinner. Happen you all made your mind set on a time to go home?"

"This evening come sun-down," Dena said. "I already told Waits it'd be a hundred weeks e'er I put all in rights, so he said to come on home and leave you tie things together."

"Hit would be *me* had to."

Homer stopped the fuss. "Seems you might recollect this is your last hour as sisters," he said.

Quick tears came to Bess. "I never aimed to act ugly," she said.

"No more did I, either," Dena told her. "Must be it's the thick hotness."

And with peace helping, they got the house froshed up again.

In the late summer evenings the hills around Glen Hazard are no longer purple. They are the steel-blue of a new gun barrel and, when the sun goes down, the earth is lean, and the tired trees are quiet, and the moon is a mirror in a flat sky.

Dena and Bess were on the porch, and Dena's eyes were taking a long look at the friendly hills.

"I might maybe see Big Wolf Bald again, and I might maybe come and go many times, but after this night it'll not anymore be home. There's the orchard I've sat up with on freezing nights to keep the smudge fires burning; and the fields you and me tended."

"You've fretted at it all a heap o' times," Bess said. "A person might think you'd be glib to be free. Hark to Waits, a'ready! Wonder could he learn me to whistle like he does?"

But Dena went on, unheeding: "There's the single trace path down to the spring, where I've carried water since scarcely bigger than the bucket. All the place will look different where I only visit at."

Then their eyes came to rest on Waits Lowe, now come so far as the gate, and calling to Dena: "I'm standing here!"

He was sun-browned from the long summer, restless as ever, dark and eager, and Bess had a fear that even a wife-woman might not hold him long; and what about Dena if Waits should take another going-off spell? Yet this minute she was leaving her homeplace to go with him. Bess watched her sister and she could see her content and ready, but Dena's feet were fastened to where they stood, and when she smiled on Waits, it was as if he was a mile away.

Waits called out again: "I'm standing here!"

"Stand there a while longer," Dena said; and she went in to make a farewell to Homer.

She and her father were close in their thoughts and ways, and her heart was all knotted up in her, to see him sitting there, crippled and shrunken. And she was sorely gramyed over this going.

"Waitstill's come after me," she said, while she stood before him.

"Come back and see us, gin you can waste the time," Homer answered, as he chopped at his tobacco twist as if it were a stick of waste wood.

Bess ran in to get her old sweater, ready to walk with Dena so far as Lowe's to see the going home, but when she came out again, there was Fayre Jones talking with Waits, and so polished up that he was perfectly strange. So Bess slipped back once more and changed to her Sunday coat.

Dena was in the doorway, with her back to Homer, and looking as if she wished she'd not been wed. She called back once more: "Waitstill's come after me."

"Best follow him, or dark'll overtake you," Homer said, whittling tobacco all over the floor.

Fayre Jones loped up the pathway, bent his head under the door lintel and went within to make his manners to Homer, and when he came out he spoke to Bess as if he'd only that minute noticed her.

" 'Lo," he said.

"What's the use of you?" she answered him; and they followed after Dena and Waits and took the path beneath Cragg Hill.

It was a gentle going, and each of the four let life run across them, making patterns as the leaves made dancing shadows in the westering sun.

Bess looked at the two in front and then up at the long, thin boy beside her. She was pledged to him, surely, but what might their going home be?

And right on top of her thought, Fayre said: "Well enough for Waits Lowe that he heired to a homeplace for his wife-woman, but where at am I going to keep you? A lone man like me gets perfectly embrangled studying how to come by his needs."

Together they came to Lowe's cabin, under the

shadows of Cragg Hill, where Rashe and Barsha Lowe stood at the door waiting. And when the young ones drew near, the women stood aside together, with their eyes gathered upon their men, and Fayre and Bess kept far back.

Rashe and Waitstill stood upon the step by the door, and Rashe said: "Son, this house is yours, and this land is yours of right, for it falls to you on behalf of your grandsir's grandsir, your grandsir, and me. I have nought to do hereafter with any land, saving enough to bury my body when I die."

And so deeding the homestead in free gift to his son, Rashe stood down from the step, and took his place, homeless in the world, by Barsha's side; and Dena left Barsha and stood upon the step by Waits.

Now Waitstill put his hand in hers, and the other hand he stretched out to his mother, while Dena gave hers to Rashe, and they drew the old folk within the doorway. And Waits said: "Welcome to this house, so long as you need a home upon earth, and the Lord grant the years many."

And Barsha made answer: "Son, we are yours to care for and cherish."

And she kissed Dena, and went quietly after her

into the house, to take second place thereafter in all things.

Dena and Waits now came out of the house again, looking as if they felt more like thieves than not. And Bess ran to her sister and they clung in each other's arms for a long minute, till Bess said: "Never you fret over Homer. He'll do finely."

"See you give him the top cream," Dena ordered her. "And watch you'll not neglect the chicken-birds, with me not there to prompt you."

Fayre and Waits shook hands for the first time in their lifelong days and Fayre began to say: "Wish you happy . . ." But it sounded queer, so he only said: "I'll fetch down Dena's things soon as Bess gets 'em together, gin you'd leave me do it."

And Waits said: "Kind thanks." And they kept on shaking hands, neither knowing how a person left off, for it was an unusual thing.

"Hit's latening, we'd best get back, Fayre Jones," Bess called.

So they made farewells and trailed off, and all was awkward as may be.

Fayre and Bess were back at Howard's Place before either found words, and then Fayre said: "I'm bound I'll come at a place for us some way."

"Where'd be the sense of it," Bess asked, "and me disabled to leave Homer? There's not a person on earth could tear him loose from his homestead. Hit'll end up with you living right here soon as we get wed—if so be I content my mind to take you."

Fayre let his eyes take in the house, and the good level fields; and Bess could see his mind making itself up back of his wide blue eyes. After long enough he said: "Reckon as well not. Never would we come to rights as to which was head-leader of the place. Time I get me a homeplace, Homer's welcome to dwell with us, but that'd be different."

"Meanwhile," Bess said, "here I stand, wasted betwixt you two stubborns."

CHAPTER IV

FAYRE JONES, in the dawn of the next day following, was by Big Gully graveyard, studying on the hardship of getting cash money to buy a homeplace, and he was all folded up on a log, whittling at a snaggy stick, for a man may not think and walk at the same time, but a knife and a piece of wood starts many notions in the world. He had got no further than wondering why all a man's troubles run back to lack of cash money from the start, when Waitstill Lowe came toward Glen Hazard, shouting and singing and full of the glory of life.

"You're a early one up," Fayre greeted. "Been over the hill to help the sun out o' bed?"

"I got Dena home!" Waits chanted. "And it's a hot day and a gold mist, and the time soon coming when the leaves let go! And I got my wife-woman safe in my own house—gars a man's heart rise mainly proud, and . . ."

"Be passing along," Fayre told him. "Every man on earth ain't wed yet."

"Never you fret. Likely you'll come at a place; and Bess'll get her mind set, saving she don't see some chancier man than you."

"You got a masterly way of taking other folks' trouble light," Fayre lamented.

Waits was ready to help out with sound words, but he never got to it, for a powder blast went off so near them that it blew all else out of mind.

"Let's us brogue over 'n' look at the road-workings," he said, while Fayre uncoiled himself bone by bone and stood over above him.

Below Big Gully Hill a great wound lay along the side of the slope, dripping red clay like blood on the green scrub, and in the end of the gash was a huddling of busy roadmen and their tools, like maggots gnawing. They squirmed around and burrowed under a great boulder that lay next the path, and directly were wriggling up or down the mountain side out of harm's way; and the foreman lighted the fuse and went running back down the gash as fast as his legs might take him. The second blast roared off, and the boulder was a scattering of rocks spurted into the air. Gravel came flying up so far as where Waits and Fayre were standing.

"The wide open road's close on us," Waits said.

"Wonder me what-all the gang's aiming to do gin they get so far as Howard's Place? The survey crosses the old trail right over his homestead, and he's in no manner glib to leave them have throughway. He's been forenenst the road since long along."

"Homer's that set on his orchard trees," Fayre said. "Been raised with 'em."

Now the misted sunlight was made ugly by the shrieking of the great steam-shovel that bit nearer to the old farm with every scoop of its hungry mouth. The boys watched the derrick clank back and forth. The engine-house spurted jets of hissing white steam, and the rattling scoop spit the mouthfuls of hillside down the lower slope, while each fresh bite bled drops of earth. It ate the last safety betwixt Glen Hazard and the Outside, and it chewed with a sharp rasping sound.

Waits Lowe turned up his collar against the noise, as if it struck him like a cold wind.

"End of the week," he said, "and they'll have ate clear up to Homer's fence line; and then they'll be up against what can't be blasted off with powder."

While they looked on, the hot morning crept over them. No rain had fallen for above a month, and the air was burned and dusty to the taste. The long heat had squeezed all the rich smell out of the balsam trees, and it was like drinking syrup to breathe them. There was no cool place even in the heart of shadow, and through all the woods was no sound of running water.

"Heard you whatever of the upscuddle in town night forerunning yesterday?" Fayre asked.

"September's a colory month," Waits purred. "The summer green has started to fade to different kinds of browns and yellows, and the sun slants so it shows all the colors of the bark and moss."

They listened to the noise of the workings where it roamed through the hills and searched out the echoes. And in due time Fayre said: "You got queer eyes. Come you tell it out, I see all that as good as you. There's a power of difference betwixt us that way. I look at a tree and say, 'There sets a tree'—a oak, or gum as may happen. You see a tree and you carry on about it a fright, and talk for a perfect hour, just like I never asked you ary question."

"About did I hear the town's fuss? Me, I loaned a hand in it. Time and past that the road gang was scarce of theseabouts."

"You're a scandal," Fayre said. "That's no way to act, and you freshly wed."

"There's news about Bess visiting with Morris Ott," Waits said. "Woman persons is mighty easy-hearted to a man that's hurt."

"Maybe you'd tell me to go break a leg?"

"All is you take a wise word from me, and watch that flitterbudget of yourn don't get embrangled."

"Hit'll take till back end of the year to get a homeplace and fixments."

"Take her the while she's yourn and do the fixments after, like I done Dena."

But this did not rest with Fayre's mind. He said: "There's another way we disfavor. I'm the planning kind, and you're the happening kind."

"A mort o' things come to pass the while you're making up such mind as you've got," Waits warned him. "But likely we'll both live till we die."

"Was ever a time you and me had like notions since cradle-days?"

"Never was. Hit wonders me we'd not chip out o' friends."

They moved slowly on their way to Glen Hazard, while the big mill whistle screamed that dinner hour was come already.

"Funny thing," Waits said. "Such times as you think other to me—you're only different. Ary other man took such contrary notions, and I'd say he was wrong in the head."

"That's what being friends is," Fayre told him.

And half a mile later he said: "I picked me out Ansen's farm for a homeplace."

Waits stopped short and took time to laugh at him.

"You talk about 'planning' and then you pick a house a'ready lived in; and you with not a coin of money to tempt Nels Ansen with!"

Fayre Jones leaned back against a handy tree, and Waits perked his head on one side, ready to hear what his companion might say for his foolish self.

"I fail of being a busy, fighting man like you," he began, while his quiet eyes looked solemnly on his friend. "But it's unbecoming in you to make a mock of me that's not got ary homeplace nor folks. What I get I got to strive and figure for, while things come right for you. There's times, Waits Lowe, when I come close to hating you."

"Times you come close to spoiling a pretty day," Waits grumbled. "Never aimed to trample on you, nor I never said you'd fail of coming by Ansen's

Place. You and Bess is properly mated—neither one of you can abide being made sport of."

They went forward together, but the sun was dull and the day had no more life in it.

CHAPTER V

ANSEN'S PLACE lies at the foot of Big Gully Wash in the hollow southerly of Cragg Hill, and between Howard's Place and Glen Hazard in such way that it is over against Lowe's cabin, only Cragg Hill stands betwixt them. A man may go up Cragg Hill and then, beyond Gillow's spring, take a right turn down to Lowe's, or follow his left hand to Ansen's.

This early morning Fayre Jones went by the high road the better to inherit the sun, and he was eager with hope, though truly he had scant cause. He carried his loose-hung length gaily up the hill, with his wide blue eyes alight, while the brisk wind whiffled his hair till it stood six ways. And he was as homemade a boy as ever trod the walkable ways.

When he got over the hill's crest the gusty wind struck against him, and he sneezed sharply.

"The wind's a heap catchy about now," he told himself. "A man starts out warm, and the first he knows, he's studying about that coat he's left hanging on a peg back in his house. I'd ought to drink me a dose of cold-curer time I get home, and stop this afore it starts."

Under the deep blue sky of Indian summer the hills were softly gray, and the near slopes were sprinkled with purple flowers of Michaelmas daisy and ironweed, and with the old-gold flowers that come to hearten the world in the late fall. The wild morning glory was blooming again, all in and out the snake fences among the bryony, and tall grasses stood up bravely, stretching their spires high and proud before the first frost should break them.

Fayre poured himself over a fence and trailed down the left-hand path until he came out above Ansen's Place and looked down upon it.

The homeplace he craved lay spread before him, a most pleasant farmstead resting in the soft, gold light. And here he was, waiting for it to be his, for he rode lightly on life holding himself ready for the next happening. Always matters came to pass hardly for Fayre Jones; and when he had to bestir, his head went mixed, and his mind took pattern from his hair and pointed different ways.

Fayre sat him on a broken-down fence rail and thought about this farmstead. Above twenty years he had lived in this world and never had a homeplace, so it seemed to him the most contented thing a man might get. He had been hand-raised with the Joneses and as a consequence never had learned what his proper name might be. Years since, they had gone down to Fentress, and sought to take Fayre, but he had clung to Glen Hazard; so his scattered boyhood was watched over by Barsha Lowe, and Aunt Matt Ewart, and the Howard girls' mother before she was by.

The fence rail gave under him, and he picked out a sounder one to sit on, while his mind roved across the desirous fields. A wedded man is bound to have a house for his wife-woman, and a garden piece for his young, and some fields besides for raising a living should work-wages fail.

He studied Ansen's Place.

The house, when he looked overly close, was a poor thing, yet it stood on a southy slope, catching full sun, save that it was overbraedened by a grandsir white oak for shelter. The barn was newly raised, and there was a shed and some leaning outplaces, and a fenced yard for the hog. All the place was run around with a snake fence, and held in a hill's curve safely. The high fields were not uncommonly tilted, and there was a low pasture on the side where Never Fail Creek ran broadly.

"I pointedly had ought to get me this place," Fayre said aloud; and he went on redding it up in his mind. "Over yonder's what is left of a orchard. Maybe we might tickle them stumps into growing us a apple, gin our saplings get rooted. And then I'd take 'n' fix up that gap in the blackberry briar, so as the children'd not fall in the creek and in a manner lose."

He stopped and looked at his words, and said: "Seems my mind's run a far piece, contriving for young-uns a'ready, and me not yet wed. But I'm a planning man. Waits Lowe, now, he'll just study on the fine pretty world, and every child-thing that comes to him 'n' Dena'll be a surprise. Me, I'll get this place set up proud—supposing, o' course, the man it belongs to is aiming to sell it. I wonder me, is he?"

Fayre got off the fence and started across to where, on the further field's edge, a man was bent to the work of turning last weeds under. And while Fayre climbed down one slope and up the other, he watched to see how the land had been cherished; and he was glad it was freed of rocks and trash. The land had been stump-rooted, save for a few left here and there to hold the earth where it might wash away in a storm of rain, and the slant places were held with covergrass.

"Them Swedes is clever farmers," Fayre owned. "Does a place good to be tilled by 'em."

There was a humming sound from the far field that might have been near bees or a far-off buzz saw, but when he got closer Fayre heard it was Nels Ansen who made a song to ease his toil.

"Good day and a fair sun, Mist' Ansen!" he said.

And Ansen stood upright and stopped singing, and looked upon him with eyes deeper blue than Fayre's own, serious as a child, and waited to hear what was.

"Hard farming on this slant," Fayre went on, "stiff ploughing, and a poor turn o' soil when done, I reckon."

Ansen said: "Ja!" and he wiped his red face, and stroked his bright moustache and smiled so that his teeth showed a fringe of gleaming white.

"I make out," he said. "For a man to live is anyway hard work in the world."

"They tell me about river-bottom farms where crops grow a sight in the world in ready-made soil," Fayre told him, "and flat land, moreover, that catches a power of fresh soil every rain that come, in place of washing out poorer."

Ansen bent to his work again, and he said: "I have heard so much."

"A pity it is for a man to uneasy himself scratching at a downgone place like this is, when there's land down Grassy Cove that'll yield of itself, and not a heavy price either," Fayre went on.

Nels Ansen straightened up and took a full breath. "I cut my weeds a little off," he said.

Fayre lingered in the slow hours, and shummicked back and across the field, or balanced on the fence top, while Ansen chopped at the stubborn weeds and ploughed them under.

In the late morning Ansen rested on his plough and said: "Is it a visit this is? We go in house."

Fayre said: "I'll be broguing on. I got my work, same as you got yours."

"That is better," Ansen said. "Winter comes."

THEN Fayre made his way aslant Cragg Hill, over by Gillow's spring, and down so far as Sam Ewart's, for it had come into his head to visit with Morris Ott. The goodness of the day brought the notion that it was a denial to be housebound, and since he could in no manner get forward with his own affairs, he might readily do a kindness.

The morning's cold wind had gone away, and in the noon's dusty stillness it came to Fayre to wish that Morris had broken his leg at some nearer place, but by means of keeping on he got at last to Sam's house, and all were at dinner.

Sam hailed him in the high voice that was a surprise, coming from a big and sturdy man.

"Pick a chair and pull up," he squeaked. "No need to lack, so long as we got plenty browsing."

"I come to visit with Morris," Fayre answered, "yet I recall me now of feeling hollow. Kind thanks." And he fetched a chair to the table, where Aunt Matt had already placed a sudden dish for him.

She dodged back and forth the house, carrying Morris Ott his food, or fetching coffee, hot from the stove.

"Feeding folks is the thing Matt does best in the world," Sam excused her. "Nothing'll cure her of making bearm over it. Matt, set you down! Here's Fayre with news to tell, and can't for the racket you make."

"How was you knowen I got news?" Fayre asked.

"Anyway it's feeble. Only I been studying on a homeplace and picked out Ansen's."

Morris Ott's voice cried out: "Talk louder; I'm wishful to learn what is."

Sam Ewart gave himself seriously to the business of dinner. He was a heavy man and bone idle, but kindly as Aunt Matt herself, though slow in mind. He rocked along peaceably if nothing happened, for he had worked out a scheme of things for himself, and it gave him a solid look like a railroad tie. Every while or such a matter his wife-woman scattered his notions, but most times he gathered them up again and pounded along his own way.

He now said: "Was unknowen Ansen aimed to sell. For gosh sakes, Matt, set *down!* Go on talking, Fayre."

Fayre told about the place, and ended up: "Been planting selling seeds in his mind this very hour back. Got him studying about river-bottom land down Grassy Cove."

Again Morris Ott called out: "Come on in here! I got words saved up for you!"

"You keep still," Fayre said. "I'll be better company time I get dinner inside."

Directly, when Fayre was beside him, Morris

said: "Where at you got the money for Ansen's?"

"What affairs you got with that?"

"Thought maybe you failed of it," Morris answered. " 'Tain't for me to mix in. Ary news from down in town?"

Fayre cast around in his mind, and then said: "Nought to make stir. Talk about the road has about got citizens split in two, and there come right smart of a sprattle, day or more back."

"Bess Howard told where she and Preacher heard it. I reckon folk had as well get their minds set."

They talked scantly, neglectful of special words, and falling at cross meanings, since they were not overly friendly together. And time drew itself along through the middlewards of the afternoon.

"Gin all you come for is to freck a person, as well keep out o' here," Morris complained.

"Sakes knows why I put myself to the trouble," Fayre said, "but someway I can't help but spud around you."

"You're as welcome to not."

And they fell wordless again, while the sun streaks crept over the floor, and glirred up the wall, and went away by the window to leave the room faded with the coming night.

Morris came out with a notion that had been gnawing at his mind.

"Micajah Dobbs is meanest forenenst the road's going through. Longer it's hindered, the longer he'll make him three years' money in one, the way the gang makes liquor trade."

Fayre got up and stirred to and fro the room, and wondered him was it worth while being on his way. From the window he called to Morris: "I foresee Doc Peters; reckon I'll stroll."

But the doctor rolling in before Fayre was gone out, they came together in the doorway.

"Hi, Fayre Jones," the doctor hailed, "you doing any good?"

"Just tolerable," Fayre said. "When you aim to leave Morris run around?"

"That depends as it happens," Doc Peters answered, while he went into Morris's room. "I'll not be long here should you care to bear me company on the back road."

So Fayre filled in the passing time listening to Sam Ewart saying many words, and when the doctor came out again, he called to Morris: "A quiet good-night to you!" And they set out to get townwards.

"What was Sam speaking about so much?" the doctor asked.

"Never noticed," Fayre owned. "Had a thing of my own to plan for." And he told about his craving a homeplace.

When he was done, the doctor said not a thing, but his silence was so urgent that Fayre said: "Come out with it."

"Rightly, it's none of my affairs," Doc Peters began. "Only me being in the medicine business, I can't help but notice. Happen you'll not stop drinking, there'll be no homeplace, or anything whatever."

Fayre was taken all out of breath.

"Me?" he said. "I never did use liquor, not to say commonly."

Doc Peters walked on. "Like I said," he told Fayre, "it's not my place to fault you; only I wish you well."

"Heap o' folks call me simple," Fayre said. "Maybe I am. Always I been a poor hand to quarrel. Give you good-night!"

"Here!" the doctor ordered. "That's me, back and front, taking up a story at the wrong end. What I mean to say is, there's more poison in them package bottles you buy for drugs than in clean corn liquor. Thought maybe you're not aware."

"Give you good-night," Fayre said again, and this time was properly away.

"There's not a thing ever I do that falls out right," he thought bitterly. "Come I aim at a home-place, Waits Lowe's got to make sport. Come I visit with Morris Ott to be neighborly and he gets out o' manners. And now here comes Doc Peters poke-nosing into what kind of stuff I take to spry me up some. Must be it's envious he is that I fail of having him write a remedy for the all-overs."

CHAPTER VI

THE citizens of Glen Hazard made talk of the wide open road, when they were widding around town's center after the day's work was done. They were gathered in the place to the number of half-score, and among them Virgil Howard, and the Bart Brothers, Newt Beechy, and Fayre Jones—all waiting until No. 11 southbound should run. The fast express never had lingered in Glen Hazard in man's memory, but it might be flagged any day, and meanwhile it was a neighborly thing to see it on its way.

Work on the new road was all in a caddle, due to Homer Howard's stubbornness, and the highway makers were in sharp sprattle among themselves for the mistake made in starting such a work before clear through-way had been signed. The State men claimed the county had prepared the way, and the county failed of showing papers, so all was in a knot, and the laborers, being idle, were a scourge to the hill country, the way liquor trade thrived and their camp over against Big Gully was a noise and a shame.

Among the townsmen only Newt Beechy stood out for the road, and this just to be contrary. Newt was gant and leather-faced, and built so he was bound to say "No" to every other man's "Yes," for he was a fozy old man and feckless.

"Efn it rested on me," he began, "that road would go slap through Homer Howard's Place and bust it in two halves."

"Homer's a helpless cripple," Virgil said, "and moreover he's cousin kin to me; and I'll not have his homestead bust in two by whatsoever roadmakers."

Luther Bart said: "A road lets in the outside, and gin it comes to pass, a power of hurt's liable to run in and destroy us."

"I seen in the paper," Fayre Jones said, "where, do we leave the road come through Glen Hazard, it might likely do a power o' good—getting garden truck to market and such. Given a rideable road we'd be at Four Mile Switch right now."

"What ever time we got ary leftover truck saving maybe to swap with next neighbors?" Virgil asked, sampling an apple from the basketful Newt Beechy had forgotten to put down.

A questioning growl came from the Glen Hazard men.

"The paper furthermore said," Fayre went on, "where the Robbins' Gap people crave the road to run through thereaways."

"Leave 'em have it," Luther Bart said. "We've not got ary thing to tote out saving corn liquor, and there's not a thing to tote in but what's worse. Move over, Newt, and leave some other man space to stand." He helped himself to one of Newt's apples, and complained: "Always under foot, you are!"

Talk drifted slowly. Almost they could see the words spreading and fading like smoke in the air above them, for Indian summer lay warm on the land and pressed heavily. Young Ed Gillow, lately back from his school in Massengale, was using a cigarette, and it so took up his mind that he sat and looked down it with crossed eyes and had no part in the talk.

"See that foolishness," Luther Bart said. "There's a piece of outland a'ready. A man had ought sooner to eat his tobacco than set it afire."

Preacher Howard started another notion: "This ain't no common road. 'Tis all unliken the county road, where taxes may be worked out. 'Twill call for cash taxes from every last one of you."

Sharp talk now broke forth, for pay-taxes were strong against the road, and these had not been thought about till this minute. The pale sound of No. 11's whistle mingled with their discontent.

"She's so far as White Oak," Ed Gillow said, while he crushed out his cigarette to be ready. "Look where Uncle Shannon Budd goes!" he cried, pointing to where the old wastrel was weaving down the hill over against the railroad. "He's drunk as a fresh-boiled owl."

Newt Beechy said: "The days have gone by when new things should send us to our hid homes back of the spurs. We're bound to go on, or we're liable to die out."

"Sooner that than have the misery a wide open road is liable to bring with it," John Bart made answer, while he reached over and took one of Newt's apples.

Fayre Jones was just stretching out to get him one, when he gave over, and raised a shout and started off running, for Uncle Shannon Budd stepped across the tracks as if he had all the time in the world, just as No. 11 came screaming around the bend.

"Uncle Shannon's what you might call mirk drunk," Luther Bart said judgmatically. "Here he goes in the face of an evening sun and thinking it the midst of night."

Fayre jumped for Uncle Shannon and jerked him aside, while the citizens went on eating apples, and No. 11 fanned past, with the engineer spitting curses out of the cab window.

Luther Bart was yet speaking, though some of his words had been lost in the train's rush. "The way that old trash heap will step a knife's width in front o' death is fitten to turn a person's mind loose. A accident likely will overtake such carelessness one o' these times."

Uncle Shannon's faded blue eyes were innocent in his red face, and his trailing white hair made him look almost a wholesome citizen, only his clothes were scarcely fitten for rag mats.

"I'll thank you to leave hands offen me," he complained to Fayre, who was steering him along, "me that ain't got a soul to keep me from being jerked around by whoever. Not got ary mother, or daddy, or brother, or . . ."

Fayre sat the muzzy old want-wit down on the corner of Ranson Gillow's store porch, where he went on lamenting, while Newt Beechy stood over him saying harsh words to his face unchided.

"Fayre Jones's legs is too long," Newt said. "He'd ought to left you linger on the track a extra spare second and we'd have had a nice funeral to excite us."

"Oh me, oh my," Uncle Shannon groaned, "and me with not a soul; no mother, nor . . ."

Now the train was gone by, the townsmen began to scatter to their homeplaces, and those who had distance to make were lamenting being kept so long.

"A person had ought to write a postal letter to that engineer," Luther Bart quarreled. "No. 11 come five minutes late. Soon she'll not be along 'twel come dark, and then what'll we do?"

FAYRE JONES came out of Gillow's store with a bright green package of drug medicine that claimed to be good for the trembles.

"Stepping in front of fast trains ain't specially wholesome," he told himself, while he went along slowly, and his mind groped among mixed thoughts. There was the thing Doc Peters said other evening, about medicine being poison. Couldn't be at a dollar and a half a package; that was out of all reason, specially when it made him feel spry and brisked-up. Yet maybe had he put the money by and hoarded it, it would have done as much good.

Making long steps up the hill and beyond, he tried to figure how many years of weeks it would need to save up enough out of wages to get him the homeplace. And in such manner he came so far as the new cut, where the earth-scraper stood up like a black demon keeping watch over the devil's work, and Fayre was so deep in his own figurings that the sound of a trampling on the road back of him caused him to jump wide.

But it was only Preacher Howard who rode by on his eternal white horse.

"A night's rest to you!" the old man called.

"And to you a pleasant waking," Fayre said; and the Preacher rode on, he and the beast uncommonly large against the falling sun.

The sky was yeasty with clouds that spilled over the hills and broke the last slanting light into sudden shadows. Looking ahead, Fayre saw where the Preacher's horse had taken a distaste to the earth-scraper, the way he ambled sideways and began to fancy along the trail. And the Preacher's voice came back along the road: "Sho-up, Jolter Head! You 'n' me's met the devil abroad in these hills afore this. Sho-y, sho-y—'tain't but a new devilment!"

And when Fayre's long steps had brought him up to the Preacher, the old man said: "Who'd fault a beast—such a looking object would make a person himself prance. I trust and pray that Homer holds out a while longer. Gin you're that way in, you might 'ware him how a man's liable to get horse-throwed. Well, another good-night to you!"

When Fayre turned in at Homer Howard's Place, he was not best pleased to hear voices, for he had craved a homesome time. None answering his call, he trod up the path and looked in at the window. The forward room was full of moving shadows that the lamplight cast from the men that fretted around Homer. And Homer himself was wrapped in the pool of light in the midst of them. The wrangling voices of the roadmen came out to Fayre, and the foreign talk, gusting forth in sudden, sharp words rasped his ears.

Fayre crept around to the back door of the house and in at the kitchen place, and there found Bess by the inner room. She was listening and her head was all in a spin with eagerness.

"Little more and they'll win him," she whispered.

Fayre took her in his arms and kissed her solemnly; then he set her aside and went forward.

Homer bid him to a chair beyond the firehearth, and Fayre could see the battling light in the old man's eyes. He took in, too, that the roadmen did not know how close they were to winning.

Homer was stubbornness come alive. He rested quiet, and soaked up all the men said, while one of them waved a long white paper before him.

And now Fayre sat him down and said to Homer: "Strange days we're getting for the time o' year."

"Uncommon strange," Homer answered, easing down in his chair.

"Been ne'er a frost yet."

" 'Tis so, there ain't. Green winter makes a fat graveyard."

"How'd your apple crop come out?" Fayre asked, with manners.

One of the roadmen broke in, "See here, we've no time to be standing around while you . . ."

"Bid you good-day," Homer said peaceably.

The man said harsh, useless words.

"Not deaf," Homer said gently. "Hit's my legs that's weak. My ears ain't crippled any, I thank you." He went on: "Happen you think noise is sense. But I'll not be yelled into giving you through-way. O' course I'd be glib to have your money—but home's home." He looked at Fayre.

"Home's home," Fayre agreed.

The head roadman tried again. "See here," he argued, "why don't you buy a place down to Glen Hazard with the right-of-way money? You could do that and have a pile left over from what I see of the dumps."

Homer said: "Ur."

"Look-a-here, having the road come right slap through is going to double the value of your land on either side, leave alone the price you'll get for the strip of highway."

"There's no sense to double the worth of properties that ain't for sale. Hit fails of reason."

"You can't farm this place, the way you are, and no more can't your girl. What good is it to you? I'll bet it don't earn more than bare keep the year round."

"Ur," Homer said.

"And in poor years you'd be a heap sight better off in town."

"Ur?" Homer asked.

"There's sociableness," another of the men struck in. "You'd not set alone, weeks in and out, but you'd be right in amongst neighbors."

"Ur!!" Homer quarreled.

He said it so uncommonly loud that both men were silenced.

The chief took a fresh breath.

"You can sit there saying 'Ur,' " he shouted, "but this road's going through, if you take your money or not. We're paid to put it through and through it'll go; and after that you can claim on the county for what you'll get—which will be small. Take or leave."

"Ur," Homer said sadly.

Bess now came to stand back of the chair where Fayre sat over against the old man. Homer looked across at her.

"Time for your say," he told her.

She craved to tell him: "Leave the road through and be done—soon or late it'll eat its way—as well strive with the weather." But it was hard to take part with strangers to gainstand her own father.

Fayre said stubbornly: "You'd best keep fast hold on the homeplace."

And his meddling so far discontented her that she went over to Homer and told him: "I reckon you'd as well leave 'em have it."

"You hear what your daughter says," the road man cried out. "Now she's a young woman got sense. She sees it will be like I said. . . ."

"Bid you good-day," Homer said, as soon as he could make his voice heard.

"Well, all I say, Mr. Howard, is—we got through idling around waiting on you. Men and machines is eating up funds. Come we finish off the Big Gully cut, you'll be condemned. I'll offer you just five minutes more to sign. If you want compensation money —here y'are."

Homer looked at the right-of-way paper, and said peevishly: "I a'ready told you one time this last hour to give over wiggling your fool papers in front of my eyes."

And then, when the road clerk had nearly got them nested in his pocket, and was turning to the door, the old man sat up and said, on a suddenty: "Here—hand 'em to me! Bess, fetch a pen; Fayre, lift that ink bottle down offen the fireboard; hand me a book to bear down on!"

They stirred to do his orders, and all gathered

around. Fayre was misput and miserable, the road-men were grinning like a hantle of pumpkin heads, and Bess was only excited. The fire jumped up to see what, and seeing all peaceable once more it then settled down again.

Carefully, slowly, Homer traced his name. He held the paper up to the light and waited for it to dry. He had Bess put by the pen and ink, while he looked dourly on the men who were in a twitchet to be gone.

Then he jerked the paper into the heart of the fire and the flames ate it up eagerly.

"That'll learn you to come flapping your papers around me," he said. "Bid you good-day!"

The road clerk fetched home his hand that was yet stretched out to take the signed paper. He opened his mouth, but for the first time in long along no words came forth. And he went out and his men with him.

When the strangers were gone away, the three looked on one another for long minutes. Then Homer dusted off his hands, and Fayre laughed out loud to see him sitting up pert as a pepper bush.

Homer said: " 'Tis safe burned, and my signing with it."

But Bess took the sulks.

"You're a pair of—of—of *menfolks!*" she said, disabled to think of a worse name.

CHAPTER VII

THEY rested quiet for a long hour, feeling the place safe about them, warm and homesome after all the bearm. The very walls were fellowly, drawing close as if almost they feared the threat was not yet gone away. Only the fire, excited by its bite of lawyers' paper, was jumping and leaping.

"I took all the trouble to come up here to tell news," Fayre began. "I found us a home-place."

Homer was thinking about his trees. "Come spring, I'll chip some o' them sourings with russets," he chirruped.

"Pity it is I give over the notion of wedding with you," Bess said to Fayre.

He stared at her in a maze, for this was a ruinous thing.

"Hit don't set with my mind."

Homer said: "Efn you all aim to get in a sprattle, I'd as well lay me down. A'ready my ears is wore out with foolishment, and there's small pleasure harkening to you young-uns. I'd thank you to carry me off."

So Fayre dragged him away to bed, and when he got back by the fire, he said to Bess: " 'Twould be hard saying what did agree with your mind."

He looked her over to see whether she fitted into the new home he had picked out. He could only see it in spring time, with the apple trees out in flower, and Bess, scarcely more than another apple blossom, playing at being wifely, while himself did all the heavy work. He hoped there'd not be ugly winter days, or much rainy time, for she was such a fledgling of a thing.

And while he was shadow-haunted with why Bess never got a hand's-grip on life, she said: "The world's builded upside down."

The fire snapped and darted, and looking at it Fayre said: "In the dry back end of the year a man might put fire to the woods and see it burn so far as Massengale, happen the devil sent a favoring wind. Some ways I fear you've gone tindery that way. Set light to you, and—poouah!"

"I hope," Bess said, with serious eyes watching the flames, "I hope my dying will be no more than a flicker. I hope the Lord'll blow me out like a candle."

"We're talking about wedding, not dying," Fayre told her in temper. "Keep your mind on what I'm telling you of Ansen's Place. There's a sharp chance o' grain on the fields. You 'n' me might raise us a wholesome crop o' corn, and stock and childrens. And you could keep chicken-birds besides."

Bess said: "I'm sick o' crops. Dena never talked of a thing else."

"But listen here, Little Thing," Fayre said doubtingly, "we're bound to raise crops efn we have young-uns—you'd want young-uns, Bess?"

Bess looked for a long time into the fire, and then she said: "I'd like better'n anything on earth to have a dress the color of sun-shadow on snow."

Fayre was gramyed and all in a misery. "May be I'd get you that—but you'd crave child-things?"

"Reckon I would," she owned. "But I doubt me could I keep up with them and chicken-birds both."

This freshened up Fayre's heart, and right away he was talking again: "Gin I get a ax and saw on that old house, and a fresh plank now 'n' then, it'll do finely. The barn's ripe new, and the outplaces not unseemly, and the hog pen . . ." He slowed down when he thought about that, and ended up: "Well, maybe we'll not get us a hog right at the start."

Bess had a dread of such talk. Not a thing to see all her days but a house and its needs. And when all was done, there it was to do over. There was no end to such matters. The road going through might have caused some stir, and now Homer had quenched that—the old stubborn!

"Who's going to pay for all the fixments?" she asked.

Fayre only said: "I got a plan. I'm a planning man, and I can see a power o' distance."

Bess scorned him. "You maybe can outlook a power o' country," she said, "but I can't see you any nearer inheriting any of it. Times I think I'll take off, like Waits Lowe, and go view the world. Stories he tells makes my heels twitch."

This very minute she ought to be sewing on Homer's shirts, for the mending was already piled up beyond hope. "All I crave is to be glad," she thought, "and matters rise up in my head to quarrel at me. Hit's a sadness the way work things rise up and spoil all the fine pretty days." And she kept still, hoping the shirts would forget themselves, but there was nothing else in her head. Not even Fayre Jones was a comfort such times, since he would be only another man to be sewed and cooked for. "As well stay here with Homer," she thought, "the way he flies out in a spasm gin I so much as talk about being wed."

There sat Fayre on the far side of the hearth, just the way he'd be for years on years after they had a homeplace, with his shadow snooping around back of him and striving to get away betwixt the chair rockers. He was pleasant to look at now, the way his eyes were dark hollows, and the firelight showed the shapely edges of his face and turned his hair all coppery. She studied about him being an old man, with his wide mouth sunk in back of a white beard.

"Looks ain't all is to a man," she puzzled, "yet saving that some's better-favored than others they're all just about alike."

Fayre stirred as if he was on edge to speak.

"I trust does he say a useful thing," she hoped. "Does he make common words, I'll turn loose and say what's on my mind, and that'd fail of pleasuring him."

The fire slept fitfully, winking now and then and jumping up like maybe a person that won't own he's dozed off; and then settling down again until the room was nearly black dark. And over the fireboard the tall clock clucked and clucked while time was gone away.

Fayre had at long last found words.

"Hope to shakes you ain't going wandery," he fretted. "Some men's got to, but 'twould be a jeopardous thing for a woman-person. There's a power o' living to be done right here in Glen Hazard."

Bess flamed up: "Maybe you fail of being knowen how a woman wants out. You never figured the times I just stand looking at that stretch o' dirt road that runs up to Sunview and beyond to the outside, and hate it for going away 'n' leaving me here. I hate the trains that cry out in the night, carrying folks up and down the land, and me forgot on this little old downgone farmplace!"

Fayre opened his mouth, but before he had time to get words out, Bess tore on: "You think wedding with you might content a person. That's the measure o' sense you got. I doubt me is it such a joyful matter to be wed even when all be easy, but when you got to live poor thereafter 'twould be perfectly graceless. There's got to be a chance of living, and a homestead, and so much gear as will keep life in a person.

Plain out, Fayre Jones, what'd you do with such as me?"

He was altogether fashed and woeful.

"All is," he said, "you got a frecket fit."

Bess yet went on: "All the years you been knowen this farmplace, did you fail o' seeing I never learned a thing toward being a wife-woman? Dena's that kind. I never did keep in head what next to do, and with her gone this place is liable to turn slom over. Where's next spring's crops to come from, with me unknowen so much as what seeds to get?"

The clock shivered, and sneezed eight times, and when it was over the spasm of time, she said: "I got it in head to go to city places and work in a store."

"Great forever!" Fayre said, "to think o' the mort o' years the Lord used to make this piece of earth fitten for you 'n' me, and you go outgate your wits craving to grab all the balance of the earth as well."

And then he unfolded from his chair and came over, bodaciously out of temper with all this; and he took Bess by both shoulders and shook her sternly.

"Drop such talk, hear?"

Then he lifted her up and kissed her, and made such a solemn business of it that she was quiet.

"All that brabble a while back," he said directly, "was only talk. 'Taint for you 'n' me to make any matter of it."

"Maybe 'twas only tired out I was," Bess owned.

Fayre was content. And he said peacefully: "We'll get wed soon's ever I lay hands on enough cash money to buy off Ansen's."

Bess drew herself away from him, and shook her head mournfully. "There's yet a hard thing to edzact."

"Tell what is."

"You come 'n' got pledged to me, calling your name 'Fayre Jones.' Come to find out, you've got no rightful name. Happen I'd join with you, I'd be a mock, and not be proper wed at all."

Fayre leaned against the fireboard, tall and shadowy in the red glow.

"A man's not handily to be faulted for what come to pass ere he could speak. Supposing I fail of being knowen my proper forefathers, I'm thankful to them that raised me and loaned me a name to be called by."

The way he had answered her made her ashamed; and she wanted to hide her face against his coat collar and tell him that a name made no matter—but a person's got to have some pride. So she only said: "I ain't faulting you. I never aimed to say a hurtful thing."

"Ain't hurt," he lied gently. "You just talk to shadows. Man that's got no name fails of being a person anyway."

CHAPTER VIII

A HANTLE of days thereafter, in the thick of the afternoon, Fayre Jones came shogging over to Sam Ewart's house, and Morris Ott saw him from far off, for Morris was sitting up against the outside wall of the kitchen side, with his useless leg stuck out on a board in front of him.

The world yet failed of rain, and everything was so tinder-dry that a person scarce dare think about a match. Through the haze of dust the near slopes were blurred, and the sunlight fell sleepily through the lazy air. The very breeze was unwholesome, for it came warm and sickly, and only moved enough to rattle the belated leaves that clung to choking trees. A rain-crow was giving warning in an uncommonly rusty voice; and odd times the bird stopped as if he listened for the fat, slow raindrops that should come lumping down with the splat, splat, splat that gives promise of an onding directly. And when they failed of happening he called again.

Since Morris Ott's leg chained him down, his mind

was more than commonly eager, and the devil now sending Fayre Jones his way, Morris began to mix a dish of trouble.

Fayre stepped across the mill yard, dodging scrap wood and broken metal, getting a piece of bale wire cleverly around both ankles and raising a stir of white dust with every tread.

"How you frogging?" he called when he came near enough.

"Well as otherwise," Morris told him. "What's the time o' day by *your* clock?"

Fayre fetched him out a kitchen chair and mounted it back to front as if ready to ride off on it next minute.

"I got a groping pain here and there and don't sleep to do no good," he owned. "Where at's the folks?"

"Sam's gone off in his wagon to fetch him a new saw from the freight office. Aunt Matt's back in house—you hear her."

Aunt Matt could be heard withindoors singing in a high chirrup that a grasshopper sat on a railroad track singing polly wolly doodle all the day. And when Fayre went in to make his manners he found her fossicking around in odd corners, counting linen things and making up her mind about which clothes would do another winter and which were ripe for the scrap bag.

When Fayre was come out again, Morris said: "Unlucky thing you're feeling sadded, with all you got to do 'n' earn this fall. Must be you got a fresh almanac with new diseases in it."

"What I come to talk with you of—Bess Howard said where there was a thing you said."

He stopped and looked at Morris with troubled eyes; and he ran his fingers through his dusty hair. A man got dry all over and parched out, toward the end of a summer. Even his mind was powdery, so that the least puff of a notion might scatter it.

Then he finished his words: "You're the one that set her on asking me questions, I'd not be surprised."

"And supposing I was," Morris answered. "She's got a right to be knowen who she's wedding with. More especially gin he's got no homeplace."

And then, of a purpose to stir Fayre up, he said: "Neatest, prettiest thing in Glen Hazard, Bess is; mouth just made for kissing."

But Fayre only tilted his chair back and forth and spoke sleepily out of late memorv: "Made for kissing, maybe, but firm enough in temper. Bess don't keep her mouth shut to amount to much, but gin she does so, why, help the man that gars her open it. The next words'll be hot as pepper."

From where they sat against the house wall, they could look across the mill yard to the shed, which was no more than a roof on gant poles cross-braced. The upright boiler of the steam engine, the saws, and the shafting all stood out black and hard against the pale sky beyond, and the rest of the yard was filled with the copper-colored light of coming storm. Over back of the southerly hills the sky had gone the steel-green of standing water.

"There sets the same boiler tank that got Waits Lowe in trouble. Recollect the time it fell on Burl Bracy's foot?"

"Echo is scarce dead yet," Fayre said.

"Calls to mind Micajah Dobbs," Morris went on carefully.

"Micajah's a man fit to damage belief in human beings," Fayre answered.

Morris yawned and stretched back in his chair, and spoke lazily of the road gang, and how its going would make an end of Micajah's trade; and how the road was a threat to all Glen Hazard.

"Happen the road gets ruined, the gang'll be a sharp time putting it back together again," he ended.

"Reckon so."

"Now I got a thing to show you," Morris said, while he sat forward in such haste that his boarded leg slid off its chair to the ground and he howled.

Fayre picked it up again skillfully and contrived so to rest it that Morris said: "Some ways you're handy as a woman-person. Kind thanks. Now, listen and hark to my words. 'Cajah Dobbs is glib to pay cash money to whosoever ruins that road."

"What man would be liable to?" Fayre asked.

"Dummock!" Morris said. "How'd I know? I'm only just saying that's what he's ready to do—cash money."

Fayre did not properly take this to himself until Morris had spilled enough words to set his mind awash, and this matter used up time.

"I never favored dealing with such," Fayre said.

"You're mighty choice for a no-name!" Morris plagued him.

And Aunt Matt this minute coming out with a pitcher of lemon drink and some spice cookies, they gave over serious talk.

Morris said: "Aunt Matt, gin I say to you, 'Go

ruin that wide open road'—what'd be your answer?"

Aunt Matt stood with the pitcher held up to offer a glassful to Fayre.

"Me?" she said. "I'd shape at it, even did I do no better'n make a mongle."

"I'm took aback at you," Morris laughed, "and a good go-to-meeting woman like you."

"Hit'd be a surprise what I might do," she said seriously. "I ain't one to meddle-'n'-make, but come I study on what mischief that road's liable to lead in from the outside—hit gars my hair grow out in tangles."

The sun was burning a hole in the edge of the mountains, where he might hide him for the night, and the smoke from this burning covered the world.

Fayre got up and said: "Hit's darkening, I'd best make my way."

"Stay longer."

"No, guess I'll set out."

They watched him lope off till he was out of ears' length, and then Morris said: "Pity it is a sharp one liken Bess got to wed with a dull one."

"They'll match," Aunt Matt told him. "Fayre's got more to him than even himself is knowen."

And suddenly she peered sharply at Morris.

"Young-uns forever!" she said. "I declare efn you ain't craving Bess Howard your ownself. Love 'n' young-uns 'n' trouble all go about together!"

"Hit's a denial to be crippled up here with doings going on," Morris grumbled, while he reached out for his hickory crutch.

"I'm well-hoped this weather'll happen directly," Aunt Matt said. " 'Twould, efn that fool crow had his way. Storm-threat breeds trouble." And she trotted withindoors with the pitcher and glasses jingling a tune.

The green light faded to gray, and when the copper sun had gone away there was no after-wind to cool uneasy heads. So Fayre felt himself pushed along by the heavy air, while the far sound of thunder snored behind the hills. It rolled in his head and tumbled his notions over and over.

It was an ill thing to deal with 'Cajah Dobbs any day of the year; yet money to get Ansen's Place he must have.

"Saving only for my dubersome name," he fretted, "I'd not go near such trash. A man lacking all I lack is a sorry person. He ain't scarcely free to choose."

By the time he came so far as Glen Hazard, homely lights filled the evening windows, and children with happy shrieks played *Run, Sheep, Run* in the darkling corners.

"A man's bound to have a place to keep his wife-woman in," Fayre reasoned pitifully, while he lingered to watch the younglings.

Soon he was gone along the up trail, and there was now no sound save his own footfall on the hill-side, and the crazy popping of shrinking timber back in the woods; and Fayre's heart was lonesome within him.

CHAPTER IX

Down from Wild Cat Ridge into the Dark Corners rode Micajah Dobbs upon his wastrel horse. Micajah was a sorry being, put together in haste of such scraps as were left over from proper men, and it was a surprise he did not shake to pieces with the rough going.

He took a hid path that ran snaking down the slope and lost itself in a dry stream bed until a mile or such a matter. Then he climbed out on the ledged rock, the way the horse might leave no hoof-marks, and went into the laurel scrub where no path was—but Micajah could keep the trail by the set of a far tree, or the twist of a low-set scrub, or by the way a rock overhang cut the sky.

And going up a narrow trace, he came to a hole in the hillside and there slid down from off his horse and went forward, first giving a signal-call that any within might know who came and leave him enter in safety. A whistle from inside the mountain told him that Dite Morgan was there already.

Inside the hole a rock-walled path led back and crooked around a bend, and at the far part of the bend it opened into a cave place. A red glow showed in the cave, where was smoke and fire and the black shape of Dite Morgan crouching. There was a rock furnace with a kettle atop; and a groundling spring was turned to run through the tub where the worm lay coiled; and the liquor dripped into a great vat. When the smoke from the fire had gone through a short rock chimney, it spread and thinned in the passage, and its leftments got out of a chancy crack, so never a breath of it would 'ware the officers the way to Micajah's still.

Dite Morgan, who now sat back against the further wall with his knees drawn up and wrapped around with his arms, was filled with a restlessness that stirred the frousty dark. He was a square and heavy boy, with a pleasant-made face that had altogether gone to waste. There was no more evil in Dite than in a potato, and no more sense. And his eyes were earth-colored in the scant light of the furnace fire.

Micajah stretched himself along the rock wall over against the fire and breathed the wholesome steam in great content.

The first while they used no words.

It had been a rich year, with the whole kenning of roadmen craving freshening, the way they slaughtered trees and flung boulders from the way; but with the joining of the road at Sunview Pike the men would be gone from theseabouts, and trade thereafter would shrink up as in the small days.

"Hit's a waste—Morris Ott being damaged," Micajah said at last. "Time we best could use him, there he sets down at Sam Ewart's looking like a thing that's been mail-ordered and not called for."

Dite said: "Morris give promise to send Fayre Jones in his place."

"Fayre Jones ain't fitten to put weight on," Micajah complained. "Moreover, I'm not one to favor getting the place kittered up with persons."

Dite got up to heap ashes around the edge of the fire where it was creeping, and he said: "Never did figure it out, but Morris 'n' Fayre recall each other in a person's mind."

Micajah tasted the liquor. "She's coming too fast. Tastes thin. Smoulder the fire some."

And when he had licked his front finger dry, he went on: "Morris 'n' Fayre is nearabout as like as water 'n' fire. One's got dark eyes and is short 'n' hard-set, and 'tother's got blue eyes and is long 'n' loose-strung as a stream o' water. That's the kind o' mind you got—to liken 'em."

"They favors a heap some way you can't figure," Dite argued stubbornly.

"Pity me for hiring a lackwit," Micajah mourned.

"Fayre'd be handy for putting blame on should there come a happening. Gin it got fastened on him, he'd run off sooner'n be mixed in a fight. That way we'd be rid of him and the road both."

Micajah's head nodded back and forth for a long while, as if once set going he was disabled to stop it.

"I'd put more dependence even in you," he said directly, "but the law's took such a distaste to you and me both that it'd be unhandy for us to be mixed in a mischance. Should harm come to this niggling road, we'd best let some other take the weight."

"Morris Ott tells where Fayre's altogether mis-put for cash money to get him Ansen's Place."

"You could 'a' said that earlier and been a help," Micajah grumbled, while he stirred himself and made ready for a trip up to the roadmen's camp over against Big Gully. "Me, I've cast my eye over that properties my ownself," he ended.

He set forth, and Dite Morgan, left by himself, let his mind follow Micajah. There was a sharp back-debt owing, and likely it would be in the butt of the felled tree hitherward of the camp clearing. Micajah would stop there and come back with the fruit of the dead tree heavy in his pockets. Dite's mind slid on to Fayre Jones. It was cheerful thinking about the road being spoiled, and even though most likely he'd have all work to do himself, it would be a wholesomer thing to have folk suspicioning Fayre—the way he'd be the only man seen around.

The warm darkness overtook Dite, and the next news he was aware, here was Micajah back already, and Fayre Jones with him, and they were at ripe words.

"Happen you'd not aim to do all like I ordered," Micajah quarreled, "you've no claim to come sneaping in these localities. Apt to get embrangled is what you are."

"I come on up," Fayre said, "since it was my debt due to a harsh promise to Morris Ott. This place smells sour. I never aimed to get caddled up with outlaw doings."

For answer, Micajah pulled out the earnings of that day and cast them on the ground. He said: "That's but a smidgen to what I got holed away. 'Tis a good trade—gin we cause the road persons to linger."

Fayre looked at the money and thought about his needs.

"I bet you my ears . . ." Dite Morgan began. But Micajah said: "Sush, lunkhead, there's enough words spilled a'ready."

So they sat back in the shadows against the wall, and Fayre was alone in the glow of the firelight—he and cash money striving together.

Fayre asked the money: "What all would come to pass *after* such a happening? Supposing I made a bobble at it and got me jailed?"

But the money so far out-talked him that directly his mind was years ahead, and he and Bess had long got the habit of dwelling on Ansen's Place. Corn stood heavy and high on the low fields, and apples were swelling on the trees, and there was an early fire withindoors.

His eyes lifted up to see only the fire in Micajah's cave, and two men were watching and waiting for his mind to set.

Silence came like a piece of glass, and he kept pushing at it without seeing what hindered him, until he was all blown about by wretchedness. He recalled: "When two forks lead to the devil, take you the middle road"—but he failed of finding any middle path. Between his "Yes" and "No" there wasn't room for the point of a needle. This thing was trag, besides being a risk to deal with Micajah Dobbs; yet how else to buy Ansen's?

Micajah stooped forward and stacked up the bills and silver pieces, and when all was away he said to Fayre Jones: "You got to be helpsome, gin I let you have the least coin."

And Fayre humped himself together and shivered as if the fire might have been cold.

And then he answered Micajah Dobbs.

"A man's got to have some place to keep his wife-woman in," he said.

It was late along when they were done talking, but at the end of all Micajah said: "You meet with me and Dite up at Big Gully come mornglôm."

And Fayre said: "I'll not fail you to be there."

And Fayre came out of the cave's mouth into pit-mirk night, and had trouble in plenty to find his way out to the right trail.

CHAPTER X

THE Dark Corners have weather of their own. There is a rich dampness there in the driest times, and a nervous wind rattles the low-set scrub when the rest of the world is quiet. While Fayre got down to the hollow below Micajah's cave, the crooked shadows hid along the trail and leapt out from shaking bushes, so that often he stopped to see if any person was there. And finding none, he gave over being jumpy, for he had no fear of empty darkness. And when he went forward it soothed him. His mind glirred over present miseries, and again he saw himself at Ansen's, content with Bess. And he dreamed of these coming days when he should give all sorrows to the dark heart of the years. And in this manner he came in right time to his place beyond Big Wolf Bald.

Fayre's house where he lived alone was no more than a one-room shed with an earthen floor. Years past a house had stood handily by, but that was long burned. When he had lighted his lamp there showed only his bed and a table, and a turned-over box that he used for a chair; and on the table was a mixture of things. In the stone hearth were cold ashes of the morning's fire, and beneath the fireboard hung a skillet and a tin coffee pot. Far in a corner beyond the lamp's circle was the gleam of the washtub hanging like a nightmare of a lost moon caught indoors; and in another corner a ghostly broom. Fayre might be forgiven for craving a homeplace. Yet this long-forgotten wood-shed was home to him, and in it he had been content.

He now gave a thought to supper, but there was poor heart in the notion, for muckering with Micajah had uneasied his stomach. He recalled that he had work to do. There'd be time enough to eat after that. A man might relish a bait of beans with such a matter behind him, and he wondered him what eatments he might be fedded should he land in jail. And this so embroiled his wits that he drank the most of a bottle of medicine that was on the fireboard.

Next he lifted the tub off the wall and bailed water into it from the nearly dry rain-barrel just further of the back door; and when he had bathed he rubbed himself dry with half an old blanket.

"There'll be towels when I'm home with Bess," he said aloud, "and sheets on the bed, likely."

He turned out the lamp, and slid among his tossed blankets.

And being ready to lie wakeful, he was asleep forthwith. But he woke up during the strange middle hours in a white sweat, and with nerves so teased that they caught the least sound; and he lay a longsome while hearing unusual noises.

For a sharp time thereafter he was quiet, studying on what the Lord might think of such survigrous goings-on, for Fayre held tight to a simple faith in a good Lord who does most puzzling things, truly, but is mostly at hand when a man's in trouble. In a gray mist that was neither sleeping nor waking, Fayre lay and watched his mind search former times for peace.

There was a day when he and Waitstill Lowe had fallen to ructions about this, and the matter grew so serious they took themselves to Preacher Howard that he might judge. Waits was argüing that the Lord never had done a thing for Fayre Jones, and where was the sense of Fayre putting dependence where he'd been let down; and Fayre claiming that he'd hold on until Waits showed him a better.

Fayre brought his mind back, and heard a new wind combing the trees. The night was stirring. He thought about Micajah's cave and heard again the whispering of the money and saw it on the floor in the firelight, but when he got so far as to tell Micajah "Yes"—he saw, instead, Virgil Howard, sitting on his porch steps; and in front of the Preacher were two boys, all hot and tumbled from their quarrel. Virgil Howard was a forceful man and his word was the Lord's own. Over the faded years his voice came sharply: "There's no one remedy to heal all that tread the common walk of life. Waits is the questioning kind—and he may as well question. Can't do harm and may do good. Fayre's the following kind, that's bound to have a thing to clutch hold of. Fayre Jones, you keep holding."

There was a further matter, and Fayre, now broad awake, fought for the words. They slid across his mind like the shadow of a flying bird. He climbed from bed and looked out of the window for them, but they would neither speak nor let him alone.

Outside, the night began packing up to move out

of dawn's way, and a great rushing about and tearing around she made over it.

"May be will come a storm o' rain," Fayre hoped. "The kind o' storm a man can't leave home in."

The window was a blue square now. Time he should be getting started. The notion not to eat he now saw to be a foolishness. And when he was clothed he made a bleak breakfast off cold bread and apple butter, and washed all down with the balance of the medicine.

He said: "Even supposing this bests me, 'twould be better'n being called scared to try—or would it?"

The Preacher had one time said that a person ought to be sturdy enough so's he'd not fear being called a flinch. Fayre thought about this, and first it made sense and then it failed of reason. And without any explaining whatever here were the mellow words of the Preacher: "The Lord's never failed me all my years—though times His notions and mine were varying. The Lord's mighty reliable."

Fayre brushed the breakfast scraps to the floor, and swept all into the firehearth with a ready broom.

He said: "Anyway, I got to keep my binding word to *meet* with Dite . . ."

Then with a lifting heart he went out.

The wind cracked like a whip-thong, and the world was barren. The edge of the morning opened yonder of Glen Hazard, and Fayre trailed endlessly toward the gray dawn.

But his head was hot inside and as he walked the trees slid by him with a strange gliding. The next hillcrest was within hand's reach and then it was a mile away, and he misdoubted of ever getting so far as Big Gully with the world moving back and forth. When he passed Howard's Place it was yet fast closed. Most likely Bess would not be out of bed yet. She'd be surprised directly.

He looked over to the road-cut for the others, but it was yet too early—unless that shadow glirring along the far crest might be Dite Morgan. Fayre crossed over to the new cut, slipping on the dew-wet clay of the fill. But there was no one. The big road machines were asleep, and he touched the harmless jaws of the earth-scraper, and drew back from the cold bite of the iron. His feet were laden with the red clay and every step a weariness, so that he thought about himself being foolish to have come around this way, and sat him down on a handy rock to clean the cumber of mud from his shoes. He sought about for a stick to scrape with, and his eyes came to a piece of string that snaked from a bigger rock beyond. The end of the string was afire.

Fayre looked at the little bluish curl of smoke going straight up in the rock's shelter, perfectly the picture of one of Ed Gillow's fool cigarettes. He looked down the cut, where it lay in an even grade, dropping in long, open curves right onto Howard's Place. Did a slide happen now, half the hillside would dump all over the farmstead. His eyes came back to the smoking string. A blast would set the whole road sliding down. These two notions came together inside Fayre's head with a crack.

Fayre's mind moved slowly, but his legs were built for speed, and he was away from his rock and tumbling up the side of Big Gully in no manner sure of the going, but with the need to lose himself from there racing through his head.

A struggling mass of noise was piled upon the earth, as each following blast made deeper the seamless thunder of the sound. Fayre lay where the fright had flung him, while chasing echoes scrambled through the hills seeking for what had spoken. He held his breath until the last shudder of the world was spent, then warily he raised his head.

Fayre looked toward the road's end, where a slide from the hill had come freshly down, and at the fill which had gone down the low side, covering trees and scrub so that only their tops stuck up through this new red blanket like sprouting weeds. Far below the bank lay the steam shovel, its cabin half buried in the earth and the biter taking a last useless mouthful of trash.

His eyes sought Howard's Place and failed to see it. He sat up and winked, he stood up and stretched his neck—but there was nothing. And he crumpled down again, for his arms and legs shook master and in no manner answered when he called on them to give over, and his head was blank as a house moved out of.

Shouts and the clap of running feet sounded on the road behind him, where the whole skail of citizens from out Glen Hazard were come to see what earthquake had taken place. And black figures poured over the crest beyond as the roadmen gathered from their tent camp back of the ridge.

It was a chancy time for Fayre Jones to be gone away. Instead he stood stuck where he was, searching beyond the ruined road and seeing not a thing but chaos. And while the men of Glen Hazard, shaken from night into the lap of a stirring day, ran and stumbled over the tossed heapings, Fayre's mind began to come back to itself, his body came alive again and he crawled through the scrub close along the fence around the graveyard till he could hear those who passed on the far side, and peering under the laurel could see their legs flicking by.

Some of the oldsters, long since disabled for running, hirpled along as best might be, and Ed Gillow came racing back to them, crying: "Hit's buried Homer Howard's Place!"

"Serves old Homer right," one said. "He'd ought to have been knowen the way his mind pointed."

"Time's getting on when that old man's due to be buried anyway. As well it should come to pass."

Fayre's mind was filled with fearsome pictures. Homer Howard smothered on his bed—Bess trying to get out of the house and blocked by the hillside—the house crushing down upon them—both of them stretched in homemade coffins—and himself following to the graveyard. But a man ought not to run at a funeral, and he was running now in great leaping strides.

He dodged around a straggling group and one

said: "Must be Fayre Jones is a sound sleeper, or them stilts o' his would have got him here before this."

The morning was now fully come in pale white fog, and the dew was caught in spider cradles among the brush. There was a wet crackle of twig and leaf beneath his feet, and a showering of mist-drops from thrust branches. Out of breath and scunnered with fright, Fayre drove forward to the edge of the clearing, and then swung wide and took his way across the far slope and off toward his homeplace.

FAYRE tramped on through the mist of that early morning, while his mind jumped this way and that. Between the blast that sent him scatterwit, and his craving for a proper homeplace, there was nothing save ghosts of people and a heap of mud and uprooted trees. He tried to get hold of what all this might be, but failed of recalling it. His eyes were dry and burning, and his hands stiff with dried mud, and surely he had not started unwashed from his house that morning? Time to go home now. But he no longer cared about where that shed might be. Might not be safe to go home, happen whatever he had run from would be waiting for him there.

For long hours he went on without anything in his head until his legs gave under him for weariness and he stretched full length where he fell, and woke in the light of a burning sun greatly mazed as to what he was doing here in the woods.

He sat up foredone and mull-headed and recalled that he had been running from a great noise of a powder blast. He could tell readily that he was over toward Clear Fork, and it came to him to go on so far as Preacher Howard's. Likely he could tell what the great noise was.

When he called at the gate of Virgil's house, the old man came out and welcomed him, and seeing him standing there so like common, Fayre was a little boy again come to bring some question for judgment. And he looked over his shoulder to see whether Waits Lowe might be with him as he was in the dream a while back. He heard Virgil's voice close to him and very loud, calling to one within the house, but he could not untangle the words.

CHAPTER XI

THE Howards' farmstead was half buried in red clay and white limestone, that was dotted with scattered rocks and leaf scrub. On the side nearest the road-cut, the tops of sturdy trees stuck up from the flood of earth desolated and unyielding, and the house itself was caught by the furthest lap of the slide so that it was pushed slaunchways and the roof at one end touched the ground.

The more helpsome among the townsfolk began digging cleverly at the far door that was barred by the well-housing flung across it, and Waits Lowe, who had the habit of being first at any happening, was scratching barehanded at the trash like a dog after a holed rabbit.

Uncle Shannon Budd now came up, late enough, but bearing a useful fence rail. He stopped to rest it down while he wiped the sweat from his face that was brick red from haste. And seeing Dite Morgan, he spoke out the news. "The road's broke loose," he said, and staggered on.

Dite only grunted.

There was the struggling hantle of men and the sharp crackling of timbers as the old house was prised apart; and they chopped and tore to get at those within, since the mucker was far past cobbling. Uncle Shannon came up with them, and thrust his fence rail among their legs with great good will.

"Leave me holp," he said.

There was a scream from Bess; a shrill and heartening shriek of temper. By the time Waits Lowe got her free of the wreck and dusted her down, she was saying at the top of her newborn voice, who did it, and what was it, and where was Homer, and here was a state of things.

Dena, who had run all the way from home with Barsha's shawl wrapped around her in place of a dress, tried to quiet her sister.

"Heish, there!" she said. "Quit making a sight of all of us with your racket. No person that can raise such a fuss that way is damaged overmuch."

By this time Homer had been fetched out of the house by way of a tear in the wall, and was seated in a road barrow that had been handily tumbled near his barn. There he was, wrapped about with the bed coverings they'd carried him in, and all cumfluttered with the ado, while the gathering of neighbors stood around to admire his words.

The sun got up in his due time and looked down on the biggest mess he'd seen in long years, and matters seeming worse than ever in the new light, Homer slowed down and began lamenting the mullock.

"See what come of Bess craving a happening!" he cried out. "The place was upsides of itself the minute Dena took off and got wed. Neither Bess nor me was fit to keep the place together—and now look at the consequence!"

Uncle Shannon Budd pushed himself to the front of the crowd. "We'll see you upright again!" he said. "We'll smell out who done it; we'll bring the law on the . . ."

Homer was not pleasured with this meddling. He drew himself up as straight as he could in his unhandy seat and took hold of matters.

"I'll thank you for silence, Shannon Budd," he said. "I'm the head of what used to be this house. Some person go cause Bess to cease that yatter; and you, Dite Morgan, crawl back and see can you find a thing that looks like a chair, and a pair of pants wouldn't be wasted."

All were asking one another the cause, and Ed Gillow said: "What matter is it, who caused all this? Never will it be set right, whatever man gets the weight. They roadmakers is the carelessest bunch of no-accounts anyway."

The roadmen had a hardness among themselves, and the noise of their contending rose high. The boss roared at his foreman: "Three months and more it's taken to cut through that hill and here it's to do again!"

And the foreman yelled out for all to hear: "I told you them rocks weren't anchored, and you allowed they'd hold till come next rain."

"How'd I foresee a box of sticks was left hid beneath 'em?"

"Box o' sticks! 'Twas a set blast did ever I see one. It's these plague-struck mountain men has been at it. You wait—we'll get the law down here to tame 'em with!"

And having come to this same mind they would have scattered peaceably, only one tripped over Ed Gillow and Waits Lowe and a hantle of other townsmen that misliked being called names; and this being a wholesome time to finish the distaste that started that hot day in town not so far back, they melled together bravely until Sheriff Marks rode among them and broke the fight into small rippits that drifted away piece by piece till the roadmen were harried back to their camp.

Over in a far corner beneath a left tree, Homer looked on and a parcel of old men with him, not in any manner distressed by the upscuddle with the roadmen. And while they watched they yet worried at the reason of the mischance.

"Hit's a judgment on all worldly schemes," Ranson Gillow said, being wise.

"Gin that's how come it, 'tis me that's got the judgment on behalf of other folks' schemes," Homer complained. " 'Tain't right."

"Where at's Fayre Jones?" Dite Morgan asked. "Looks like he'd be first among."

But none could tell.

All morning was given over to fetching goods from the house, and rounding up scattered chickens and counting how much was lost or saved. There was much talk and some arguing, but out of the bearm came contentment once more. For weary years the wide open road had split the town's friendship, and now the men rejoiced and came to their senses as if a great burden had been rolled aside.

Even Homer himself, being packed in a wagon amongst his things, and being a little uncertain from drinking his own health a mort o' times that day, was pleasured with the happening.

"My homeplace 'n' my orchard trees has been made a graveyard of," he said, "but maybe I'll learn to content myself in town."

"Won't be so lonesome come winter," Ed Gillow said.

"And you'll have me for neighbors," Uncle Shannon promised.

And in such manner they bore off Homer Howard toward Glen Hazard.

CHAPTER XII

GLEN HAZARD is not a specially likely place for a town, but when coal takes it in head to run out to the top of the earth, a town grows there. So the stores are fitted in handy corners and houses sprout from the sharp hillside, and if they find no natural stone ledge they are hung on the slopes and tied back with cable to trees, and their front legs driven deep in the slant below.

The company's store is crammed slaunchways to the depot; and the circumstance of Little North Fork running through this gully and not to be staunched, explains the iron bridge, built broad enough to hold the harness store and Sheriff Joe Marks' office, yet so narrow in its road space that two wagons might get entangled should they offer to pass upon it.

Doc Peters took Homer Howard into his own house against such time as a dwelling should be found. He had an overhang to sit his house on, but he never would have elected that boulder to stick out by the side and darken the window. Homer grumbled at it, but Doc said it made no matter, since he was not home enough to notice it.

The doctor was a lone man, so far as any were knowen—perhaps for the same reason he did not fret at the boulder. But he kept his house redd up as cleverly as a wife-woman could have done it: and his office in the front room was trim and wholesome looking.

It was late along by the time all were come to Doc's house, and the day so far fled that it was useless to talk about catching up with any of its work, so the neighbors stayed widding around, being wise in the matter of what next to do.

Bess was perched in the doctor's chair—himself being gone out—and she was finding this happening funny enough, being a valuable person for the first time, with all town talking about her and Homer.

Sam Ewart was more knowen than any about homeplaces, but when they put at him to say about a dwelling, he only said: "Hit's got to be in town, I reckon?"

"O' course it's got to. What good would a farmplace be with winter atop of it?" Homer asked.

"I was thinking about that place yonder of my

mill. The folks lately took out for Grassy Cove."

"That's a twisted mile out," Dena said, "and there's no manner o' use speaking about a scattered farmplace, since Bess has not got so much strength as you'd put in a thimble."

"Another thing. Come time for her to wed, where's the sense leaving Homer lonely on a new place at his years?"

"We'd ought to think about town places, only for the circumstance there's none to think of."

"What's to hinder 'em dwelling here and keeping house for Doc Peters?"

"Me," Homer said solidly. "All thanks to him for shelter till we find us a homeplace, but I'd not crave to linger where it smells of hospital; let alone sitting amongst these glass boxes full of tools gars my nerves go creepy."

Dark came before any helpful thing was found, and the neighbors took their farewell; and when Dena had to go, Bess said: "Going off in the midst of trouble makes you feel powerful wed."

Dena said: "I'll notice Waits to pull a tarpoleon over the house furnishings. They're all heaped naked down on the porch at Gillow's. One o' these days you got to catch a grip on life and quit grabbing for somebody to hold you up. Come morning's light and I'll be back to see you find a house."

Bess wiped back a heavy fall of tears that came as soon as Dena was out of the door. The day had been full of strife and she was all on edge with it.

"Pity Fayre Jones!" Homer cried out, himself not so comfortable as before the happening. "You going to take a habit of weeping every time Dena goes off? And pity me, too," he went on, "that's got only a worthless child left. Come over here and pull me near the door."

When she had settled him so he could look out over the town and watch the winking yellow lights breaking out one by one as the townsfolk got home to a late meal, he made her sit down on the door-step near him, and gentled her with his hand to smooth the sharpness from his words.

"You're my least one," he said directly, "and least ones has got to be cosseted some. You'll do mainly gin we get us settled."

"You always favored Dena most," Bess said.

And when Homer had thought about this, he told her: "Dena's the very moral of your mother-woman. You heired to all my meannesses, and as a consequence you get me riled."

So they rested in the darkness of the doorway, and the sprinkle of neighbor lights below them was a new and fellowly thing.

AFTER an unmerciful time, a house was found, and it was a place they'd failed to recall, because it had long been given over as useless. The paymaster of the coal company had used in it long since, but he and his folks were gone on to the new workings, and it now lay empty, high up on the eastward slope amongst oak scrub, and so straight above Doc Peters' house that one might cast a stone upon his roof from its front porch steps.

It had a sleepy look, owing to a broad roof coming far down over the front windows, like half-shut eyes. It was decaying under the weather's touch, and the trees crept along back of it, clustering around as if they tried to drag it back off the edge of town and take it to themselves again, the way they sent rope vines searching through the walls for a good hold. The path to it had long washed away, and a new one would have to be hewn up the slope, more like a ladder than not, with handy boulders and roots for stay-places.

Homer agreed to live there if a way could be

edzacted for hoisting him up, and Bess was eager to live in such a comic place. So the following day, with Aunt Matt helping, she went up to get it froshed out.

"Hit's been ages of years since this was a home-place," Aunt Matt said. "We're needing a grubbing hoe to sweep this floor; see them oak sprouts coming up through it! I recollect the time that coal-company woman dwelt here. She used to tell how she was mainly put about to hang her bed coverings to the sun, the way they'd go flapping off and drap on the depot and shame her."

The house had no smell of former folk, for the door had been left wide and a lot of crannies were undone. There was a double fireplace to the center chimney and a flue in the kitchen place at back. The two big rooms gave space enough for all needs and there were windows on three sides.

Outdoors, once a person got up to it, there was useful space. Although the front steps led straight down the sharp path, there was a walkable ledge that went so far as a yard on each side. The north-end yard had a wash-house and a wood-shed, and on the south end had been a garden piece, where the earth was cherished by logs built around the edges.

"I don't specially favor a house that does its growing indoors," Bess said, as she chopped and scraped at the floor. "Reckon these twisted-up old boards might be hammered close?"

"You ought to see some of the houses I've had to keep," Aunt Matt answered. She rinsed out a cloth and went on rubbing at a window pane. "Some didn't have so much as a window, and we had to leave the doors a-sprawl winter or not, so's to get light. Other places were up-'n'-down sawn stuff and so slimpsey it took a whole packet of pins to hold 'em upright come a storm o' wind."

"This place don't look overly choice," Bess said.

"Pshah! You're homesick owing to never being but in that one place you were born in—I recollect the very night and hour, and not so long ago, either. Come to think, I was the first ever laid human hands on you. But talk about homes—a place ain't nothing saving your own things is in it."

The noon whistle cut into her words, and she came over to where Bess was spreading meat sandwiches on a window ledge.

"A person that's been cleaning house gets properly eatish," she said. "Time you get friendly with this place, 'tis going to be precious living up here where you can see out. I'd not say 'No' to dwelling in this place my ownself."

They used up later hours with yet more choring, and Aunt Matt said: "Soon's you get your home things set about the way they were, all will set as easy as a old coat."

"I give you my thanks," Bess told her. "Never I'd have come at it my lone self."

"Person that's douted as many houses as me," Aunt Matt said. "Well, there's nothing! You're all swept out and ready for the seven devils if need be. I'd best be shogging home. Day's got one eye shut a'ready, and gin I fail of feeding Sam his supper, he's the scunnerest old bear ever was."

Homer and Bess had to stay with Doc Peters until the next Sunday, when the neighbor men could lend a finger to getting their house furnishments up the hillside.

Waitstill Lowe, who had planned another way of resting on the seventh day, complained that a lot too much goods had been saved from the happening.

He kept saying: "What d'you want with this, Bess?" till she was perfectly out of patience.

"What do I want with any of it?" she flashed out, looking without any hope at the mixed pile in the south yard. " 'Twould have saved a sight of care and tiresomeness if it had all been left buried. Might have been a fire from the looks; and where it all come from or where it's going to is unknowen. There's things in that mess of goods I'd forgot we ever owned."

The beds were in the center of the pile, and on top of them, fenced in by a dresser and the tables, everything else was loaded, clothes, saucepans, pictures and plates. Chairs and benches were cast around with feet in air as if not caring which way up they lay, or they stood all atilt and wobbly. The cookstove had taken up with a hawthorn bush, apart and unnatural. And, scattered from here to there, lay the strange things that fall out of drawers and boxes at moving time.

Homer himself was carried up last, by means of ropes slung around his chair, and he was placed in the empty house to await the home that should be built around him.

"Hit's a curious world," he said, when he had caught breath again after the journey and the fear of being dropped had left him, "and the longer you live in it the curiouser it gets. Never did I think about a new place at my years, especially such a bird nest as this looks to be. The water tank seems like nothing from up here, and the day I holp build it, 'twas a fearsome high task to climb atop."

"How you come on?" Sam Ewart asked, looking in at the door. "Feel at home a'ready?"

"Never felt more out o' place in all my days," Homer said, "and furthermore, soon's Bess is gone off with Fayre Jones, I know one old man that's got a sharp chance of starvation and freezing to death."

CHAPTER XIII

"FINE day!" Doc Peters greeted, while he came into Sheriff Joe Marks' office to tie up a thumb the Sheriff had ruined with a hammer.

"Fine day!" Marks made answer, balancing his arm on the desk so the doctor might get a good view of the damage.

And all who had trailed in to look at the accident said: "Fine day!" and drew close to see how the doctor got at this job of work.

The skies were dull and ugly, and the air mirky to breathe, but it's always a fine day in Glen Hazard in spite of the weather. If the sun fails, well, it's the rain that's needed for crops; and if the day is so stormy as to be outside all forgiveness, the townsmen say: " 'Tis fine for the time o' year!" meaning that any pleasanter weather would be out of the way.

But this fall, with summer stretching an old unhealthy hand over the country, the people were puzzled; and when Doc Peters presently gave out that typhoid was abroad in the lowlands, it was no more than they had been looking for. The doctor was a poor hand to give bad news ahead of time, but Shannon Budd, pushing forward to see that the thumb was tackled rightly, said: "See you keep it wrop up good. This sickly weather it's liable to canker." And then Doc was minded to give warning about the fever.

"Which gives me to recall," Newt Beechy struck in, "that you'd best keep up that ruinous cow-beast o' yours, Shannon Budd, the way she comes nozzling in other folks' spring water."

"Every person'd be wise to look to where spring water comes clean," Doc Peters said. "Clean water's our only chance."

"And how's a man to come at it," Newt grumbled, "with scarce any kind to be had, the way it fails of rain, and the tank water gone bright red, and wells all dry, and springs barely oozling—and having some person's cow in 'em half the day, moreover?"

Uncle Shannon said: "I've laid off, and laid off to fix that fence, and efn the Managing Fellow Up There will give me the least mite more time I'll come it yet. Already I got so far as planning to get the loan of a ax and saw offen Fayre Jones, he being the lendingest man."

"What's gone with Fayre, d'you reckon?" the Sheriff asked, while he tried to wiggle his wrapped thumb and couldn't. "Seems them roadmen is taking their longsome while to notice about the road damage."

"Fayre's only been up to Clear Fork," Doc Peters said. "Preacher come riding after me in a state o' mind saying where Fayre'd come in all pathery and out of sense. But 'twasn't but a spell of low fever."

Uncle Shannon Budd said: "Handy he took it the time the road igsploded, so's the weight'd not be on him."

The doctor was putting his tools away in his bag, and he left off to ask Uncle Shannon if he should wrap his tongue, while he was in the business.

Newt Beechy kept on talking in case happen some might give ear: "Crops ain't worth the slavery to gather, they're that burned out. And gin winter's creeping through the trees, what we aim to do, I ask—how're we going to make out?"

The accident being over they made ready to be out of the office, and Doc Peters was so far as the door when Uncle Shannon's voice topped Newt Beechy's saying: "All is, Fayre's a guardful man."

Doc roared at him. "Take shame!" he said, "and he the one that snatched your worthless life from under No. 11 not so far back. Fayre's as sound a man as ever went endways up; and come I catch words out of you, you old carrytale," he threatened, "I'll snap off your leg and beat you with it."

The door banged shut, and for a surprising while none spoke.

Directly Uncle Shannon spoke: "What train was that?" he asked. "I disrecall having back-talk with No. 11. I never claimed to see through rocks, but I can see both around and over 'em—Fayre's been creep-coating. Doc's a proud one to crack high of his friends."

And when the others had gone away he told the waste-basket: "Still 'n' all, Doc's got no call to be tindery."

CHAPTER XIV

IN the first week, Ranson Gillow's wife carried up Homer's dinner meal each day, because the stove, not liking the draft in its new chimney, took a tantrum not to bake. But when that was set right with a spare length of piping, and the house put forward of itself, the days soon turned so commonly that Bess found herself all distressed with household matters. Not much had been laid by for winter before the mischance, and the late year had overtaken them with scant store of preserves and dried fruits.

"Hit does look like a person's got to contrive what to eat, no matter what taking-places happen," Bess lamented.

And she took a habit of climbing down to the store to get canned stuff. And when Homer quarreled at the false butter with its hard yellow squares wrapped in paper, she asked how a person might churn with the cow rented out to Barts?

Homer said the new house had a stinging taste to his mouth, and for this reason made excuse for

Bess going something wildlike, for there is always a sharpness to a fresh home that gets in the blood and sends folk agley.

While dull days lengthened into bleak nights, he had hours of lonely thoughts wherein to call to mind his orchard trees. There was no apple gathering to plan for, and it failed of reason to forecast spring plantings now that the fields and other precious farmstead things were done away. Town dwelling was useless and dangerous, moreover; and he would come away from grievous backward thoughts to study about Bess.

"There's been ne'er a peaceful, homegrown night thus far," he said to her. "Hit's up to Aaron's Corners to the moving pictures, or worse, every odd minute. Seems you lost all hold on sound sense."

Bess said: "Supposing the neighbor boys do make me cleverly welcome. They're only such as you are knowen of—homemade and harmless."

"You're a heap too quick in the tongue, and that's a faulting thing," Homer warned her. "Seems Dena and me went to a master sight of slavery to raise you just so you might go beside yourself with careless days."

"I got to go down store."

"You've got so you're restless as a squirrel. Set still a spell the while I speak out my mind."

"Leave me go on." Bess was so far as the door, but she came back on reluctant feet.

". . . and impudent as a rabbit. The more you run around the less it pleasures you to keep house. Each time you go to fetch goods you come on back full of news where some person's asked you to go off to a play-party."

Bess leaned down and took hold of him by both ears and kissed the tip of his nose.

" 'Twould be a thankful thing did you give over being solemn," she said, and was gone in an eye-clink.

DOWN in the store she played in talk with all who were gathered, for the neighboring made her mind content, and it was the thing she had craved all her days without being 'ware.

Ed Gillow, yet free from his school at Massengale, was waiting on store this special day, and he gave her what came first to his hand, and she took the goods without being knowen what, for they spoke of other matters. Ed always pleased Bess, the way he put on Sunday clothes during week days;

so when he spoke out and asked her to go to a dance that same night she gave a ready "Yes," since he was a proud one to be seen with.

Uncle Shannon Budd, whose trade was other folks' affairs, spoke sharply from his corner behind the stove: "Gloriful gracious, Bess Howard, you'd ought to bethink yourself—taking off with persons. You'll be a scandal, first news!"

"Can't a person be on her way without tripping over you?" Bess said.

And this so tempered the old man that he took himself off, saying: "Sorry use a person getting his tongue wore out saving the young from their sins. Me, I'll go on and 'ware Homer, and see does he abide such pertness."

Uncle Shannon Budd made his way with great moaning up the path that led to Howard's, and as he went he said: "What in junket a man takes to living on tops of things for, fails me! A person had ought to stay down amongst folk. This steep's a scandal to a man's hind legs."

But he got himself up after enough toil, and when Homer had called him to enter, he settled himself beyond the firehearth and stretched his ill-begotten shoes out to the blaze.

He began: "How'd your crops come out?"

Homer waved a hand toward the valley. "They's right-sized for my fields," he made answer. "Got all fodder pulled and stored away in a teacup."

"Got ary piece of news?" Uncle Shannon tried again.

"Plenty," Homer told him. "I sit here. And when I'm all through, I sit here some more."

Uncle Shannon cast about for a way to come at what was burning him up, while he looked the place over from where he sat until there was nothing more to see.

Homer barked at him: "Come out with what you come for, Shannon Budd. There's nought so unusual about this place you need to study on it."

Uncle Shannon slowly twisted words around in his mind and at last he said: "Hit come across my mind, you'd best be 'wared of what a stir your girl's making in this township. Folks is making words."

Homer grunted.

"Take Morris Ott, for a sample—the way she's forever asking when he'll be walking around again."

Homer kept quiet.

" 'Tain't comely in her," Uncle Shannon pushed on, "first this boy and then that—skittering off to play-parties—floating here 'n' there . . ."

Homer closed his eyes.

"Where at's Fayre Jones got to?"

"None o' my affairs, nor yours either," Homer said.

"Next news you'll fail of knowen where at Bess has gone off."

"Down store, likely. She'll be back directly."

"That's the size of what you're knowen. Happen you fail of being 'ware Ed Gillow. I this minute hearn her give promise to go up to Aaron's Corners this night." Uncle Shannon combed his hair and beard with warped fingers, and looked at Homer, who yet stayed with his eyes shut.

"Well for you to sleep it off!" he cried out, "but I no more'n 'ware you what all town's saying, that gin Bess keeps on, she's no better'n a . . ."

Homer's eyes snapped open.

"Shannon Budd," he said, "long as I've been knowen you for a sneaping carrytale, I'd ought to had more sense than leave you come in my house."

"You being disabled to keep me out."

Homer drew himself tall in his chair. "Quit you for mocking a cripple," he roared. "And move you from here. Leave out from this place; and set the door wide the way the air'll get clean after you!"

The old gossip sat still.

"You hear me—outen!"

Uncle Shannon thought perhaps wisest, and he shuffled to the door.

"And me been to all the slavery to neighborly 'ware you," he fussed.

"Outen!" Homer shouted.

The door handily came open from the far side, as Dena and Bess came in, and Uncle Shannon made haste from behind it and was through to the outside.

"Where you hirpling to, Uncle Shannon?" Dena asked.

"A far piece!" Uncle Shannon told her. "All the way down again I got to go. Come for a visit, and your old man's got a pain where he keeps his temper at. Ain't fit to be sat with, he ain't." And he made off, while Dena came in to ask Homer what was, and Bess went and sat sulky on the bed.

Homer was shaking master from his temper, and it was long before Dena could make out what had come to pass, and then all he said was: "Climbing up here with his lies! I give him word-of-a-sort!"

Then she said to Bess: "Come over and own that Uncle Shannon's been giving no lies."

"As well stay here," Bess said, while she curled up on the bed.

"Elizabeth Howard!"

Bess uncurled and came over.

"You've no rule over me, Allardene Lowe," she said.

"Some person's got to rule you," her sister answered, "and Homer's disabled. Look at this," she went on to Homer as Bess stood before them. "Calls herself by the name of Howard, and then . . ."

Bess broke in: "And never shamed you. All my days long I been shut back on that old farm; not a thing but work, work, work days long. I crave to have a play time. Fit to choke a person never having a mite of fun."

Dena said: "Same place I was raised on, and I yet live."

"And furthermore I never went but when Homer give his 'Yes.' "

Homer rocked back and forth in his chair and used no words.

Dena said: "He'd not grudge you to play some. And how'd he be knowen you'd go scatterwit? Like, for a sample, you'd go with Ed Gillow?"

"That's what I aim to do."

"I order you not."

"That's what I aim to do. I a'ready told him I would."

"And you being pledged to Fayre Jones?"

"What's to do efn he takes off? He's altogether lost away, and I'll not sit 'n' weep for such trash!" And to prove this she went and flung herself against Dena and cried sudden tears.

"All is," Dena said, while she stroked and gentled her, "you'd ought to give over plaguing him. Why not you take a piece of quietness?"

"There's no room for quietness these times," Bess wailed. "I'm all tore up."

"I got to go on home," Dena told her. "You study about Fayre and the way he'll get you a homeplace. Just the way he says 'homeplace' had ought to give you sense. Hit's like it was all the world to him."

Homer spoke out at last. "Dena," he said, "happen on your way you'll overtake Shannon Budd. Make my manners to him, and say to him I'm shamed."

Bess flared up. "You'll not back down to that old worthless!"

Homer said: "Right's right. I turned him from

my own firehearth for the truth's sake, but seems I got a girl that's wild. You, Dena, do like I said."

When Dena was gone away, Bess flung herself down by Homer and said: "Always I got to be a care and tiresomeness to you!"

"You can't scarcely holp it," he said, "being born o' me. I recall my young times . . ." He stopped, and directly ended up: "You're a punishment!"

Bess said: "Never I aimed to be. Only I fail of being wise-hearted."

"No more ain't I," Homer owned slowly.

Bess twisted around and looked up at him surprised.

"Hit took a drop offen a church-house roof to quieten me," Homer told her. "Now you let that 'ware you, and see you'll not drop offen a worse place."

Bess was taken with the longest quiet spell she had had in memory. Then she slipped her hand in Homer's.

"I'll be back from the play-party come ten o'clock," she promised. "You'll not deny me to go this once?"

Homer petted her hand softly.

"You're a punishment, you are," he said.

In the full of the long evening Homer counted the clock, half hour by slow half hour, and wondered him how a helpless old cripple might lay hold on a girl-child that was bent on running with a riotous parcel of young folk.

By proper rights the year was too late along for parties, but the fall was uncommonly slow, and at each threat of shortening days the younglings made haste for one more going forth before winter storms should shut them in. But the gracelessness of the uneasy times was upon them, and they were content that the fiddle-playing was soon over that they might come pelting out into the mischievous night and spread homewards in wandering twos and threes.

Ed and Bess went among the brown trees with the late dry grass crackling beneath their feet and their blood yet tingling from the dance, till being tired at last they lingered more slowly on the steep before they should come into the town. On a far hill they saw the glow of brush piles that had been fired on the ridges and smelled the madness in the wood smoke that came soaking through the night and twisted into their minds. And the darkness being heavy around them they told each other pretty things that neither believed, till Ed asked— "Let's play being in love."

"You're trifling," Bess answered. "Think you to content yourself with one plucked so readily from another?"

Ed laughed. "Fayre's a easy-hearted one, truly, and would fail of fighting should I take what's his."

Bess dreaded that this was so, but she only said: "You crack high about other persons being flinch; but I heard tell where Fayre Jones gathered Uncle Shannon Budd offen the tracks in front of No. 11— you meanwhile using one o' them white cigarettes, I'd not be surprised."

Ed made a business of lighting another one now to save himself answering, while Bess wondered, if it came to the pass, if Fayre might fight Ed for her.

The night was haunted with cloud-hidden stars, and trembling with the half-hushed moan of dying trees; and Bess's heart was white and shelterless, drifting faltering through tired time. And this being a night of smoke and mischief that commonly grow together, she said: "Let's do a play-game to plague Fayre."

"Eagerly. The Lord made Fayre Jones to be made sport of."

When they had gone on through a long quietness, Bess said: "You 'n' me was knowen each the other from cradle days."

"We was," Ed told her, watching the smoke, "and a pleasant thing it is."

And after a further while she asked: "There'd be no great hurt?"

And Ed kissed her and gave promise, saying: "Surely no hurt. Always you 'n' me played games from child days. What folks might say 'twixt you 'n' me is nothing only voices in the wind—hear now —just voices in the wind. Only we play a game to plague Fayre Jones."

Down in Glen Hazard lamps and candles were glowing as if a person had scattered seeds of light in the hollow.

"I'm tired," Bess said. "Let's us go down."

And he answered: "We'll run down the last hill."

So they came all breathless to the edge of town and passed into the streetways. The hour was not late, but late enough to serve for talk among more sober folk. The others of the party had long since come in, and none gave greeting to these last ones, but looked serious when the two fled laughing athwart the shadows cast from neighbors' righteous houses.

When they were come to the door of Howard's Place, Ed would have kissed her again to set seal on their play-game, but she denied him, and he went light-footed down the path, untroubled.

HOMER said: "Happen a man may help himself to a wink o' sleep. You'll be the ruin o' me with all this sitting-up-ness."

"Told you I'd be back," Bess laughed at him, while the clock gave the very last stroke of ten.

And when she had got him safely away, she came to brush the hearth ashes back for the night. The fire yet burned brightly and she felt as little like sleep as it did.

"Funny," she said to herself, "funny, how moving house shakes a person up. What ails me that ary boy I'm with gars my head go feathery? Happened to be Ed this night, and he's harmless; but just supposing he'd been some stranger-person? Wish Dena was here, she'd know." She took off a shoe and peered into it thoughtfully. "I never craved to pester

Fayre Jones. Hit's just the devil comes over me. Wonder where all Fayre's got to?"

She started for bed, and turned and stamped her foot at the silly flickering fire: "He'd ought to stay handy and keep my head right ways 'round!"

CHAPTER XV

FAYRE JONES set out from Clear Fork with his body fresh and new, but yet having a groping in his mind. The stillness of a lonesome day gave no help and he felt mild and pitiful as if he had this minute been born into a strange world.

The earth lay spread in checkered browns and purples, and distant fields of stubble tilted against the hills on either hand were stitched off in crazy pattern by the black thread of fences and knotted here and there by starting rocks. The smooth gray sky arched over to the edges of the crests and all the world was just Glen Hazard and a piece beyond. Fayre trod the empty road in strangeness, wedging his body against the thrusting heavy air, and he struggled with living until it seemed he had been walking endless years with only faces of shadows on the bare black rocks for company.

Then shrill voices broke light across his misted way and dreams were born into his heart again, for now he came upon Gillow's children struggling a cow through a fence-gap beyond their spring, and the day was homesome and fellowly once more. He lent his man's strength to the halter until the beast was through. The children cried their thanks, and then were taken with a shyness and flashed away in a tangle of bare legs and blue smocks, and peeped out at him from behind the pasture bushes, calling him names to make him give chase. He folded his great length in the middle and dodged and jumped, while the young ones screamed in pretended fright. When he caught the least one and dragged her to him by a handful of her clothes, she clawed and squirmed. Half a moment he held her warm, twisting little body in his strong arms. Then he dropped her, tweaked her gold curls and jumped back into the road again to be on his way, while the children cried out: "Stay 'n' play, Fayre Jones! Stay 'n' play!"

And he might readily have done so, for Fayre had great content in child-things, but Waitstill Lowe came up on a suddenty, being on his way to work, and they went forward together.

"What business you got tinkering at that cow-beast?" Waits asked, "and acting foolish with the young-uns?"

Fayre shuffled in drifted leaves and said: "Being in love's a curious thing."

Waits gave a low whistle.

" 'Tis a serious thing," Fayre said.

"I recall I thought as much in my young days," Waits said, rocking down the center of the road. " 'Twas solemn."

"Like I was saying," Fayre kept on steadily, "hit gars a man lend a hand to ary job o' work just to be doing. And he takes notice of houses and how much they cost, and the price of things all the way from beds to butter."

Old married men such as Waits had been since the last few weeks, take no heed of such foolishment.

He only said: "Where at you been hiding?"

"Not," Fayre told him, "only I been at Virgil Howard's a spell."

"A handy time you took to be scarce, and all the slavery of struggling with Homer 'n' Bess falling on other persons."

"I took it in head to come in, searching Doc Peters," Fayre said.

Waits looked him over and raised an eyebrow in puzzlement. "Times I think you ain't worth much," he said, "and times again seems like you can't help it."

Doc Peters was gone out and Fayre made his mind set to wait, and he sat on the porch looking like the day before yesterday until No. 6 had run and Doc was back from mail-gathering.

"Come on in where there's a fire, Long Face," he said. "You sit out here taking a chill like I failed of having enough folks on hand a'ready." And when they were in by the fire, he said, "What ails you?"

Fayre spread himself abroad on the sofa, while Doc Peters fossicked around and refitted his traveling case against next calls.

When half an hour was spent, Fayre said: "There's either a heap o' matters wrong with me or else not a thing, and I fail of figuring out which. All I come for was to see could I loan a finger. You got a power of running to and from for a man as old as you." He stopped and groped around for more words and said: "Seems I might do some o' that back 'n' forth."

Doc Peters counted the little bottles before him on the table.

Fayre excused his words, saying: " 'Tain't like I was any use to amount to much."

"No," the doctor owned. "You're a proper slack-entwist. That's how come there's none in town falls in need than he cries out, 'Fayre Jones.' 'Tis a shame how useless you are."

"You make sport o' me," Fayre said. "But a man that gets called the names I do craves to make it up some way."

And when he was through with his packing and had the place cleaned up, Doc said: "Reckon you know how to pare a potato?"

"Might shape at it," Fayre agreed.

"You offer at a bait o' potatoes, whilst I fry the meat," Doc said. "I've not had a set-down meal in long weeks, and I bet no more have you."

They took themselves back kitchen and set about finding some food, and Doc lifted the stove lid and peered into the fire's leftments.

"Looks like I'm not a specially serviceable man," Fayre lamented, while he frowned at the knobbledy white lumps that he hacked into. "Either the skin fails of leaving loose or it comes out in gobs." Then he ended up fiercely, "But no man shall tell where

I'm feared of a potato." And he finished the work as best might be.

They had no more words until they were pulled up to the table, and the doctor answered saying: "To see a woman at such work, you'd think that potato peelings come loose natural."

He passed the stewed peaches over to Fayre, and said: "Don't do to neglect rightful food. Specially for such as drink strange bottle stuff on an empty stomach, and go queer-headed as a consequence."

Fayre gave a backward thought to the morning, when he'd been as lonely as a stranger in a strange land. And here he was at Doc Peters' house, natural as a leaf on a tree.

"Give you good thanks for tending me up to Clear Fork," he said on a suddenty.

"There's nothing," the doctor said, making excuse to hide himself in a drink of milk.

"And not only you, either," he said when he came out again. "The way things is being guided I fore-cast a power of fever directly."

He waited for his next words until they should come right way round, and then he spoke, beating on the table with his fork to count off the words:

"Fayre Jones, if ever again you take a dose of any drug stuff except I order it, you're liable to run off the edge."

And this being plenty to finish the meal with, Fayre offered no words.

"What is it caused you to visit with me this day?" Doc Peters asked peaceably a while later. "You got more on your mind than only queerness."

Fayre scarcely knew how to come at the answer, but after he had fitted words together in a pattern and thrown out a lot that were useless, he said: "Seems we got a thing commonly. I took notice where all in Glen Hazard calls on you day 'n' night, yet I never seen a one to be fellowly outside of your trade. Same way they use me, yet ain't got no use for me—saving Waits Lowe o' course. Times I suspicion him of being kindly more than friends."

Doc Peters hunched himself nearer the fire. It was good to rest for a quiet hour. And he turned over Fayre's offered friendliness in his mind. Doc was a lonely man, and this was the first that had come outside of his business. It was warm and grateful.

In the next hour he picked up Fayre's fellowship carefully, as if he put it in his pocket. And he buttoned his coat together over it. But all he said was:

" 'Tis an unusual thing for a young fellow to seek an old on such a matter."

"Leave that rest," Fayre said.

Together they washed the dishes, making a serious business of it and much clatter and clack; and the things that failed of coming clean at the first souse, they set to soak till another time, the way men can wash but not scour.

And when all was done, Doc made Fayre a trip up the hills to Bart brothers' to set a seal on the new fellowship and himself made ready for distance, since there came a threat of low fever already from the far-out cabins, and strangers hearing it were giving Glen Hazard a wide swerve.

CHAPTER XVI

It was yet a flat day, with a narrow wind slicing between the tall stacks of cured lumber that stood around the big mill, when Fayre Jones got back from Barts' and came against Micajah Dobbs at the edge of the mill yard. Each made a try not to see the other, but owing to no other person being in the locality the try went wide. So they shuffled on, and Fayre in a powerful fright, since he had in no way come straight in his head about the road business.

"You never was up to Bone Cave Rock that morning," he began at last.

"Due to being some place else, likely," Micajah answered.

Micajah stood only as high as Fayre's shoulder for he was a small, stooped man, crooked in body as mind, and he looked like a piece of trash blown in by mistake. Now he scrabbled along sideways, like a dog in a fit, and made such going that Fayre had to pace his long steps to keep up with him.

When they had come so far as the Company's Store Micajah spoke—as if he waited until there were other men in call, so he would not fall into a lone jower with a man bigger than himself.

"Craving is the father of all gain," he said. "Keep honing after a thing and you'll maybe come it."

"How'll I come it without you go on with this business you promised?"

"That's all used up," Micajah said.

"But I never done nothing yet," Fayre said. "All is, I was up there that morning, and . . ."

"Best lose that out o' mind. Liable to get embrangled do you say a thing whatever."

Fayre was all awash. "I'll see can Waits Lowe right this out for me," he said.

Micajah stopped and clawed at Fayre's sleeve.

"You'll not see nor talk with e'er a person," he warned.

They were standing at the branching of the roads by the Company's Store, and Fayre scowled down at this sorry little losel that came out with such puzzlements. Micajah pulled out a swelled pocketbook, the image of a poisoned rat, and took from it a bill, and gave it into Fayre's hand.

"Money comes hard but it goes mighty slick," he

lamented, while he put his case away again. "You ain't rightly earned it, but I ain't a hard man. Now put that away. A shut mouth don't let in no flies."

"Course I ain't earned it," Fayre said, "I fail of being knowen . . ."

Micajah turned from him. "Never in my days did I trade with a man fool enough to turn down money that's give him free."

Women were coming in and out of the store with their goods, and some lingered to see what might be passing hands; and school newly let out sent a shower of children down upon the town, who now gathered to see what their long friend was troubled over. Micajah backed himself against the store, for young ones most commonly meant rude words about his scattered clothing, and perhaps flung rocks.

"Put that away out o' sight," he said, pointing at the bill that Fayre yet held on his spread palm. "And never say Micajah Dobbs fails of paying his promise."

Fayre said: "You got my head all mixed. I never asked cash money from you. I only said, where at's the work?"

"A silent man never yet choked on his own

tongue," Micajah told him, and went in the store and slammed the door so hard its glass rattled.

Fayre put the fifty dollars away, thinking too late that he ought to have thrust it back on Micajah.

"This is a sweet dish," he puzzled. " 'Tain't in nature for Dobbs to pay for work ahead of time. And I ain't done a lick—or maybe I did." He thought back to the mess of happenings and recalled sitting there by that smoking fuse.

"Come on and play, Fayre Jones," one of the children called up to him, but he browsed along, without giving heed, and they trailed alongside.

Still he tried to come at it. "Some way I'm downright certain I never," he said to himself. "Only I surely was up to Big Gully that morning." Then, at late enough time, light came to him, bright as an engine headlight shining straight down the track. "Then it must 'a' been Dite I seen making off, and not ary other person could have set that blast. And me the onliest man to be seen around."

The children hung about him and called him to quit acting long-faced and come and play Tip-Cat; and they bothered his thoughts.

"And this cash money," he figured out, "is the

price 'Cajah Dobbs sets on my tongue. I'd ought to turn it right back, being I'm disabled to lay out a tale against him so long's I carry his price. Yet surely I need the money the worst kind."

He shooed the children off, saying: "I got affairs to tend, you run on. I'll play some other time."

"Tonight maybe?"

"Maybe tonight."

"Gin you get through your affairs?"

"Gin I get through. Now you hush."

So they went with him to the edge of town and left him, and Fayre kept on his way to the next hill-crest with sadded feet. Then he turned.

"I'll give it right back to 'Cajah," he said. "I ain't aiming to be bought with no cash money whatsoever."

But when he searched out Micajah in the Company's Store he was clean gone away, and all Fayre found was a kenning of mill men and their women-folk from down the tracks buying their needs and much useless things besides with this day's wages.

Fayre went on to Gillow's and there found only Uncle Shannon Budd for his trouble. And Uncle Shannon being rejoiced to have some person better than the old stove to talk to, began a long history about Ed Gillow and Bess Howard being out till a fearsome hour the foregoing night. And Fayre told him to keep a shut mouth.

"All is," Uncle Shannon said, "a man that's wiser nor you might hasten to get him his homeplace. Women is the wildest things, times they lack a steady living house. First news, and she'll have took off where the Old Boy himself can't find her."

Fayre now thrust his hand into his pocket and felt the crackle of the money. This was one time that Uncle Shannon might see more in his drink than some men with dry eyes, but he only said: "Go drown your tongue! Reckon Micajah ain't been in here?"

"No, he ain't; and he'd best not. Gin I lay eyes on that . . ."

But Fayre went out without waiting to hear what. Since Uncle Shannon's words, he agreed with himself to pay this fifty to Ansen right now, and bind him. All he had in mind was to get a safe homestead for Bess.

And while Fayre took his way athwart the hills, he thought that this was the sort of day for going to see a person and catching him gone out, and all his steps would be so much waste.

But Nels Ansen was not a moving man, and there he was upon the front porch lashing a broken plough handle, to the sound of a strange song; and all wrapped about with the peaceful smell of baking.

Fayre sniffed the wholesome flavor from where he stood at the gate, and when Ansen called him within he sat for a quiet time breathing it in. It smelled good enough to eat, but Fayre knew it took a leather stomach to make away with light bread.

"Your cooking smells sweet," Fayre said.

"Ja," Ansen said, while he went on lashing.

"I reckon you're not figuring on moving out pretty soon?" Fayre said.

Ansen shook his head, and went on singing the song to himself, with odd words that made no meaning to Fayre. He waited with manners until the tune should run itself to an end, and then said: "Supposing a man was to make over fifty dollars cash money."

"Fit . . . ?" Ansen began. "Fit-dollar not plenty roof for me, nor cow-shelter beyond and fodder yet."

Fayre told him: "I yet fail of getting me all. Fifty is just to begin, and more when I come at it. I ain't overly moneyed right now."

"Gud sends trouble to all," Ansen said.

Fayre held out the bill. "Fast as I lay hands on more I'll pay it over to you."

Ansen took it between his finger and thumb and rubbed it.

"And you see you about getting that place down Grassy Cove."

"Nej," Ansen said stolidly.

"All right, no, then," Fayre bit at him, "but it looks like you'd care efn a man had a homeplace."

Ansen handed back the note.

"I *got* a homeplace," he said, opening round eyes at Fayre.

"I mean me," Fayre explained. "You'll not keep this cash money?"

"Nej."

"Come next spring and you'll be glib to leave these parts," Fayre said, while he put away the useless note.

"Hvarför? Vår some other time of year it is."

"Maybe so," Fayre agreed, "but you've no call to talk Dutch to me, since I fail of it."

Ansen got up and went withindoors to turn the bread in the oven, and Fayre was lost in forward thoughts. Happen this time next year, he'd be sitting here, and . . . It was a hardship, Ansen being foreign. A man scarcely knew what to say to urge a trade, since the very words that would loosen a homegrown man caused Ansen to stick tighter.

Ansen came out and took up his mending work again. He was not an easy one to make talk with. He held one end of the cord between his white teeth, while his great red hands plucked up the slack in the loops. He gave a mighty pull at the last clinch, and spat out the cord, trimmed the end close, and tested the splice by trying to bend it against his knee. Then he smiled, content with his handiwork.

"This place looks powerful bony, with all leaves gone," Fayre said.

"Ja," Ansen said.

"Guess I'll be shogging off back to town."

"Godafton," Ansen said.

"A pleasant good-day to you," Fayre said dolefully from the gate.

Ansen only nodded. He was busy turning his knife blade back into its fat handle. His bright moustache frayed out cheerfully under his round nose and he went back house where the bread was cooking too much.

While he surrounded Cragg Hill and made slow steps toward town, Fayre wondered about going to see Bess. It was not the wisest day for it, nor the wisest hour, with the sun half down and suppertime around the corner. But he'd kept away these long days and he craved to hear her say where had he been, and she'd lacked sight of him, and all the thin, homesome things women do say.

Bess was gathering clothes from the line when at last he climbed the steep path, and a day's washing being more than her strength was good for, her temper was played out.

Fayre took the heavy basket of clothes into the kitchen. He went front to pay his greetings to Homer, and came back to make talk with Bess. He sat him down in a spare corner and watched her fold and sprinkle things against the next day's ironing.

The kitchen was dark with the scant yellow gleam of the lamp, and the air was sadded. The furnishments hid along the shadowed walls and in the light was only the middle table, where Bess was standing by the pan of sprinkling water, her deft head shining in the lamplight. Her striped dress and dark sweater with its collar rolled back evenly made her trim-looking and desirous.

Fayre hunched himself by the stove in a tipped-back chair and fretted the fire with a pine stick, tickling between the grate's bars and jabbing at a stubborn cinder until the stick caught alight. He played with the splinter and filled the low-roofed kitchen-place with sharp smoke. And all the room was full of tiredness and fret.

He waited to be asked his news, and Bess went on pulling and folding, and she smacked each roll of clothes into the basket as if it served it properly.

Directly Fayre began with a heavy try at lightness: "What prancing you been up to? I heard tales."

"A person's liable to, efn his ears serves him. A pretty one you are to be asking my where-ats and you out o' sight for unknowen days. You crave me to set 'n' smooch over you being away. I got the right to come 'n' go."

"So's it ain't with Ed Gillow," Fayre said. "He ain't your man."

"No more is Morris Ott, and I aim to visit with him. Leave that stick o' wood; hit gars a person's eyes sting."

"You're a scandal."

"And your ownself. I heard tell what; and gin you go scattering around with Micajah Dobbs' gang, I'll pointedly go off with Ed—there." After she had said so much she took a sudden turn. "Heap o' folks tell where it was you ruined the wide open road, but I'll not own to it. Say 'n' tell me, Fayre Jones, you never."

Disabled to find the right words, Fayre was all tangled up. "Leave me edzact it—how come it was this—me craving Ansen's Place . . ."

"Did you did, or did you didn't?"

Fayre's stick was burned down to a nubbin. He cast it in the stove and make sulky answer: "Aiming to get enough laid by so's to get us a homeplace."

"That's you forever!" Bess complained. "Didn't I get all through telling you where I failed of craving such—more especially does it spell you cootering with that gang."

The clothes were all nested in the big basket, and Bess sat herself on the table's edge and swung her legs to get out some of the ache of standing.

Fayre said: "Micajah give me cash money." And this was a thing he had planned not to say. Always he came out with words to his own damage. He thought maybe some others might be as useless as himself, only they had wits enough not to tell each and every what a lackwit they were.

Bess made no words.

He hastened on: "I aimed to give it right back. Hit was only to hush me he give it, so I'd not tell about him 'n' Dite Morgan harming the road. But I never aimed he should buy me."

"You aimed to give it back! Seems you ain't done it."

"All is I was planning to, and . . ." But never could he unravel to her how he'd worked it all out. Already it was lost in his own head.

"I took a distaste to you," Bess said. "I pointedly hate you." And she stopped as if her words had gone solid and struck against him. "That's a lie—I do yet crave after you. Happen I failed of it, I'd not grieve come such times as you make a jolter-head outen yourself. Pity it is a woman's got to care or ever she can love or hate."

"Leave that!" Homer's voice came snirly from the next room. "The way you young-uns put at each the other these days is a fright. I recall time I was . . ."

But Fayre got up. " 'Night to you, Mist' Howard. 'Night, Bess."

And he went out into the darkness. Bess went so

far as the door meaning to call him back, but the coffee took it in head to boil over just that minute and by the time she'd saved the fire's life Fayre was gone away.

CHAPTER XVII

THE back of the year was the loveliest that had been known in Glen Hazard in long memory. All through Indian summer the sun shone hardily and it was late in October before the morning frosts came and then not a holding freeze. Crops ripened early and were soon gathered. But the late heat was unnatural when it lagged into November and there was something threatsome in the soft air. Neighbors walked miles to visit with one another only to ask what was wrong with the times, and the wise among them said there would be plenty of death among the old and a great wrestling for life among the young.

Rashe Lowe, coming back from a trip to Glen Hazard, had a stern look such as a soldier may have who has heard talk of another war. He flung down the new fodder knife and slumped upon the step of the house, and watched Barsha out in the garden piece digging up the plants she was saving from winter.

"Hit's a sickly warmness," Rashe told her. "So

be the Lord sends us a snirly blast and a quick freeze we may yet be saved; but I doubt me does He get around to it in time."

"He may as well hold it 'twel I get my dahlia bulbs digged," Barsha said.

The garden piece around Lowe's cabin had blossomed heartily this year, for Barsha had a friendliness to flower-things, and she now had nothing in life but to tend them. Working in the borders and rubbing the sweet earth through her gnarledy fingers, she was comforted, and the giving over of her rights withindoors came more easily. She could boast that few old women had a daughter like Dena, who did cleverly in all things, and left her in peace in the garden.

"You'd best clean the fields close," Barsha said to Rashe. "Winter finds out what summer lays by."

"I'm no valley farmer to grudge a smidgen to the birds," Rashe answered, while he watched the crows swooping busily over his high field.

Dena this moment came back from the barn and stood two full milk-pails within the door and sat her down on the step to rest beside Rashe and to look at Barsha being busy. Dena was proud to have a mother-woman, and moreover one that had more to do than sit under foot and be waited on with grumblings, like some she had known.

The sun had long left Lowe's corner of the world, but the top of Cragg Hill was golden and the light it cast was caught in the bright tangles of ironweed around the fences, and glowed among the sage and zinnias.

They watched Barsha delving and they were silent together and the place full of contentment.

"Barsha's making a graven image out o' them flowers; 'tain't right," Rashe said severely. "Woman!" he called, " 'They that forsake the Lord shall be consumed. Ye shall be confounded for the gardens that ye have chosen.' "

Barsha said: "Shucks!"

A brisk tread sounded through the scrub, and she stopped to listen. "Waits is on his way."

"That spells eating time," Rashe growled. "Your son's too much like you, Barsha—tied fast to the things o' this world."

Barsha said: " 'Tis a handy thing you're not craving a meal your ownself. The whilst we eat, you may as well browse up to Homer Howard's old place and pull me out them bride's-veil bushes. They'll not do good in the midst of them road heavings, and they'd make a chancy hedge down here."

"That'll spare me cooking everything in sight," Dena said, while she went withindoors.

Waits now came in and Rashe said to him: "Our old woman's forsook the way. I tell where a hard frost is needed for the people's salvation and she'd put it off to cherish her flower-things."

Waits stood over above his mother and laughed down at her, while she uprooted dahlia bulbs and shook off spare dirt and placed them in careful rows in a box. "You old worthless," he said. "Wonder me how you come by such a boy as me. Must be I'm the very moral of Rashe, there."

"Out o' reason!" Rashe said. "And bride's-veil bushes is the meanest thing to uproot. Happen you might get Fayre Jones to drag it out. He's back from wherever he's been, and the mill being shut down he's got time to waste."

Barsha stood up tall and serious and waited for the aches to go out of her cramped bones, and she looked like a thing that grew in the garden and held all together. The sun was all gone now, and she was very tired. She came slowly along the path and sat down on the step by Rashe. The two old ones together in the quiet of evening with no sounds except the young ones stirring, doing the daily work that had fallen from old hands—the clink of pans from back kitchen, and the clank and splash of new water where Waits slung down the buckets; and directly a great fuss and swashing in the wash-house where he bathed himself of the day's work.

"He's got his own life to think of, and scarcely is knowen how to come at it," Barsha said.

And Rashe knew she was talking of Fayre Jones, and not of Waits, for the days were long gone by when they had to devyse to one another.

"They notice his lack, down in town," Rashe said. "They had no habit of looking on him as a serious man. But these times folks with messages to run got to run for themselves."

"None pays heed to the help of him that's over-willing," Barsha went on directly. "Fayre's usefulness is free as sun and pure water, and as scantly thought of."

"Ever since he was a bantling folk used him when need was with bare thanks, and set him aside. And best he gets gin he's away on his own affairs, is grumblings that he's unhandy."

"A shame it is. There's no willinger boy made than Fayre Jones."

After they had thought about this, Rashe said: "I spoke him 'How d'ye' a day or so back and got bit for my trouble. He was coming down the Clear Fork trail, all wool-headed. And he's gant as a hunting hound. I bid him to dinner tomorrow, it being Saturday, and he looked like he suspected poison. The man's agley."

"Hit's a sadness," Barsha agreed, "and dangerous besides. Come Waits gets out o' patience, 'tis no serious thing, seeing it takes place every hour or such. But Fayre, bless take him!—'tis time he was safe wed."

And when time had gone by, she said: "The main use of a wife-woman is to be snirly with. A man that's disabled to quarrel around home is liable to quarrel in public places, and then trouble comes."

"Old woman," Rashe asked her, "where'd you learn to be wise?"

Dena called them to supper and as they went in house, Barsha said to Rashe, "Step over by the dresser and see is that looking-glass yet working."

THE next day being a Saturday, Fayre Jones brogued along up with Waits after their work was done, and they made him an eager welcome. After the dinner meal they dragged forth chairs to the door-yard and let the day slip by them—Rashe and Barsha and the boys; and Dena, with the dishes set back of her made to set forth for Homer's house. Waits cradled his fiddle and played soft tunes, but all the brightness had gone out of life for Fayre Jones.

"Hi, Jack-at-a-pinch!" Waits plagued him. "What gars you downcast?"

"Never I thought me there'd be shadowed ways to go," Fayre said. "The day me 'n' Bess was pledged, I felt right as the sun his ownself. Now look at the way all's got embrangled."

Waits' fiddle sang a wide, slow song of sadness.

"Hit's all gone trag," Fayre told them. "First she's off to play-parties with half the township, and then sets around with Morris Ott, even supposing him chair-bound; and now matters is thinned down to Ed Gillow; and the plain of it is—I'm scared to light into him. My heart's lying all sulky within me."

"Only thing that can hurt a man is to be afeared," Waits said, while he yet played.

"Easy said," Barsha told him, "fear's the ripe fruit o' the Tree o' Knowledge."

"Then my folks never ate ary other thing years gone," Fayre lamented. "All that happens to me these days calls for a sudden man—like Waits, or maybe Morris Ott. Me, I go skwinchy just thinking about a fist fight. Worse'n that, I'd run from only a word fight. I'm a heap nervous that way. Gin I say 'Yes' and the other fellow says 'No'—there's an end of me right now."

"Paint yourself black enough," Waits quarreled at him. "Leave off insulting a man I call friend."

"There's another thing," Fayre went on, " 'twasn't 'twel you were gone off last year I come alive to know the worthless I was. You done my hardness and fit my fights as a habit."

Rashe broke into all these words, and took up where Barsha left off. "The Tree of Knowledge," he said, "is most ary tree in the world. Time you lay your ear to a tree and is knowen what all it tells, you got enough knowledge for one man to carry. Hark for a windshake, watch the moss on the bark, look at the set of the branches, and listen for the weather the winds bring gin the tree starts weaving. Knowen of that gives a man to be humble before the Lord, and breeds a wholesome fear. There's a difference 'twixt fear 'n' fright."

"Not for me there ain't," Fayre said. "I've had both and they're a shameful thing. I been afraid all my days. I prayed against it, and the only answer was weak trembles."

"All men has spells like that," Rashe owned. "No call to let it eat into your bones."

Barsha's look would have put starch into a limper man than Fayre Jones. She never had been a man, and by consequence was knowen more about them than either of her menfolk. With Fayre craving excuses for himself, all the men could do was uphold him, and the lad needing his own strength!

"Is that what you offered Bess Howard in place of a man?" she said. And she got up and went within-doors.

And none could find an answer.

Directly she came back out with an unusual bonnet on her head and a snake-stick held uprightly.

"Bess has got no mother-woman," she said sharply, "but whilst I live she'll not lack cherishing. I'm going to 'ware her she'll not take you, Fayre Jones. You ain't worth any woman's time 'n' temper."

"Old woman," Rashe said, "go indoors and take off that fool hat and fetch your patching work."

"Mumps," Waits said, "set down 'n' cool off."

Fayre made long steps to the gate and leaned upon it the way Barsha would have to thrust him aside to get out.

"No ma'am, Mis' Lowe," he said, "things ain't come to that pass."

"Whilst I'm down that way," Barsha said, without wilting, "I may as well put a word in Matt's ear. Hit'll pop right out of her mouth and pleasure Morris Ott, or maybe that young Gillow. No need for you to set on the gate, Fayre Jones. I've been over a fence before this day."

"Old woman," Rashe said, "go indoors and take off that fool hat. You heard me!"

"Hit's ripe time for meddling," Barsha went on, "gin a trashy no-account lays out to wed with a girl that is unknowen what she's getting. Hit's a sadness women's got to wed with whoever, but Bess yet has time to pick a sounder man."

"There ain't a sounder," Fayre cried out on a sudden. "I mean to say not for Bess there ain't."

"You say so," Barsha told him. "I wonder me you take your own word for it."

"Old woman . . ." Rashe began again.

"The man that calls my bonnet a fool hat,"

Barsha said firmly, "may as well buy me a better."

She marched back down the path and sat carefully down upon the edge of her chair, all primed and cocked back like a gun trigger; and the three men were silent, being fearful that any next word might set her off.

Directly Barsha pushed back her bonnet to an easier rest, and loosened the strings from the way they fretted her ears.

Rashe spoke to Fayre, the while holding anxious eyes on the bonnet: "I'll back you getting Bess free of Ed Gillow, but I'll take no share in the mess with 'Cajah Dobbs."

The homestead rested in the quiet grace that only time can lend. Where the weathered logs had grown too dark, the sun sent a splash of slanting light that startled green moss and chinking clay to life. The well-house and the door-yard apple tree pressed heavy shadows on the patient earth, and the fields were flowing gold of whiffling withered grass, held by the broad black rim of forest that was a circling cup.

"Hit's a Saturday," Waits said out of nothing.

Fayre came down from the gate, step by slow step, and watched Barsha, lest she yet take it in head to go off.

"As a consequence," Waits went on, as he picked up his fiddle, "tomorrow'll be a Sunday."

After that he played a march tune.

"Ed told me where he was leaving town come Monday. 'Tain't common news yet. There'll likely be postal letters, and such back-'n'-forth."

He finished the tune on a long howl.

"Unless o' course, Bess takes in head to go with him."

Rashe was left all behind and puzzled. Fayre gave up looking at Barsha's bonnet and turned solemn eyes on Waits.

"Soon as you got the skin peeled offen him," Waits said, "rub salt in it, good and thick, and then you button it back on him, like winter underclothes. Then you come on back here and we'll make us a play-party."

"But I like Ed," Fayre said, "him and me's been cûd these long times."

"Most likely you'd favor him making off with Bess," Waits said, "or likely you'd have her wed with both of you."

By this time Fayre was back at the gate.

"Where's the haste, Seek-Sorrow?" Waits called. "Stay longer."

"No, I thank you," Fayre made answer, "there's a matter I got to tend down in town."

When Fayre was so far away as the top of Cragg Hill, Barsha went withindoors and took off her bonnet and came out carrying her patching work. And the late sun never saw a more peaceful old woman in his longest day.

CHAPTER XVIII

WHEN Fayre Jones set off from Lowe's Place, he thought that all had come straight and was in great haste to make an end, for he suspected that what he had now in mind should be done quickly, lest he go limp.

The day well befit the going, for the woods like himself hurried without getting any beyonder. There was haste in every twig of the forest, and with every whisper of wind from the coming night the leaves struggled to be free of the trees that held them so belated.

Down in town the leftments of the road gang and the mill workers were idling away the Saturday, none settling to talk or play, but every man pacing across town if only to come back again. Fayre was taken up with his own matters and lolloped past town's center, across the railroad, by Doc Peters' house and up the path to Howard's without making answer to any greeting. Once there he was going to say his mind out for all time, and leave Bess no chance to answer back. He hollered the house, and as soon as Homer called him to enter, he fell in at the doorway and searched around for Bess with swift eyes.

"She's away over to Sunview with a crowd of young-uns," Homer said.

Fayre backed against the door as if he had been slapped, and then took himself out on the porch.

"Set 'n' visit," Homer offered, through the shut door. But Fayre had no heart for it.

There was no sense trailing over to Sunview and making himself the mock of all should he meet them coming homeward. So Fayre folded down on the porch, with the dying sun full in his eyes.

Matters had got off on the wrong foot again. When all he craved was money for his homeplace, he'd got himself scunnered; and while he was busy changing hands over that deal, there went Bess, wild as a weanling calf.

It came to Fayre on a sudden that he was making a statue of himself in the sun on Howard's porch for all town to see, and his days wouldn't be worth drowning if some of the mill workers were to take notice. "Fayre Jones setting lonesome up there the while his doney gal's gone off." So Fayre let himself down the path, and threaded among the townsmen, and after helping them wait for No. 11 he went across to Gillow's store, thinking to ask where Ed might be. But his mind jumped to the hope that Ed would be over at Sunview and it would be a waste to ask. And when he'd shummicked to and fro so long that he got himself into a state of mind, he seized the door latch to take himself inside and get it over.

The door was locked.

Fayre wiped his handkerchief all around the inside of his collar and forgave himself for going home.

"Looking for a certain person?" Newt Beechy asked, as he wandered by.

Fayre being surprised out of himself said: "Craving to come up with Ed Gillow." And the sharpness in his voice made the old neighbor stop and look him over.

"Out to settle with him after long enough time —eh?"

And Fayre wished his feelings would not write themselves plain on his face, since he'd no readiness to let the township be aware.

"Heard tell where Ed took off to Four Mile Switch on his own affairs," Newt helped out.

This was good hearing, since Four Mile Switch

lay beyond Big Wolf Bald where Fayre's house was, and he might safely set off that way and none be knowen whether he was gone home or to meet with Ed Gillow. But Fayre failed to count on the idlers, whose bones ached for a happening. In the half minute it took him to get over the bridge the gathering had plucked the news from Newt Beechy and passed it by winks and nudges, so they roared after him—"Stick law! Stick law! Pay him out good!—Polt him square athwart the nose!"

Here was a coil. Should he show himself back in town without meeting Ed there'd be a cheerful tune to dance to!

Fayre slowed down when he was safe from sight, and took his way easily. From the hollering it might be they thought him a dangerous man, or maybe they only made sport of him. But whichever way, he was promised to this job of work now, so he took pattern by his braver thoughts and in such manner got beyond the path that led off around Big Wolf to his house, and held steadily on his way.

"Gin I might work up a wholesome hate," he began—"only I plain don't think it of Ed, nor Bess either."

Further of Big Wolf Bald the road lies flung as carelessly as an apple peeling, turning back on itself nearly in circles, and then stretching out to the next curve. It dips up and down through lesser hills, first on their shoulders and then running to their heels. From the top of Big Wolf it can be seen laid out so far as Pilot, and the only straight piece is the ridge that runs from one hummock to the next as cleverly as if the roadmen had filled it; and on either side the steeps run down.

Fayre hastened to outrun the dark, and going down the following hill in flapping strides, he slung himself into the middle of the road lest he trip on a stump that stuck out from the bank. And as he went by, the stump said:

"Fall on a person! All I'm good for these times is to get stepped on by whoever!"

Fayre turned him around to look, and it was Uncle Shannon Budd, scowling from under his chewed hat and in an unhappy temper.

"I never aimed to dust you up, Uncle Shannon," Fayre said. "I got to get on and tend a job o' work."

"Was in a powerful swivvet my ownself," Uncle Shannon said, "and I started to trail Joe Marks, him being gone northerly; and come this far I give out at the knees and he kept on and left me set. Left me like I was nothing whatever."

Fayre dropped his haste long enough to ask: "Happen Ed Gillow was along this way?"

"Him was who Marks was after," Uncle Shannon said, "and I stopped and broke me some sticks to help, and time I'd got one to suit me and got it all whittled up, I started to pick myself offen the bank, and my rheumatism had took such a set that here I am for all to see."

Fayre being disabled to pass man or beast without offering aid, stretched forth a hand. But Uncle Shannon shook a woeful head.

"Chase along," he said, "you never ailed of rheumatism, so likely you fail of being knowen it can't be unfolded in haste. Takes time. I'd sooner spend the night here than be jerked up."

So Fayre took up one of Uncle Shannon's wasted sticks and went kurling down the road.

Along by the ridge he heard a double tread and stepped aside to the shelter of a laurel bush, and there came Joe Marks and Ed Gillow walking before each other and making time toward Glen Hazard. And Fayre was taken with a hot temper to see Ed in the Sheriff's hands, and from being altogether skittish of finding him, he turned in one minute to a craving to be at him.

Sheriff Marks was walking along peacefully, until a stick was thrust across the path and came sliding betwixt his feet. And Marks made a false step and was grounded on the slope head downwards so the more he tried to pull up the further down he went; and a ruined tree failing in his grasp he was altogether away, and he and the tree glirred down the slope from sight.

Ed Gillow turned himself in the path to see whither Joe Marks had slid, and while he was yet staring down, he was laid hold of and dragged furthermost the road in spite of himself.

Fayre drove his fist into Ed's mouth to stop the noise he saw coming, and with such forthrightness that he threw him asprawl. And now it was a pity that Fayre Jones was slow in the wits and not overly warlike for a little more would have made an end of Ed. But he could not handily light on a man already thrown, and by the time Ed was back on his feet, Fayre had bethought him that the sound of an upscuddle would guide Marks the way he'd trouble them both.

Neither craved the Sheriff's meddling, so they crouched together in the fallen leaves, while they listened to Marks searching for them vainly. He went back and forth a wearisome time, and then gave over—for a lone man is no master for darkness and thick woods, though he tramp till his legs grow short.

"You got a powerful way of saying 'Hush!' " Ed complained, feeling to see if his lip was cut, "but obliged to you for losing Marks off me."

They stared at one another across the edge of night, and each waited to find words. And there was nothing but the closing night and the sound of thin trees pricked by the gusty wind.

"Like I said, I'm beholden to you," Ed said at last. " 'Twasn't no serious thing, only I failed of telling Marks where I'd hid the corn I was carrying out for Micajah; and, of course, he run me up. And this recalls me, there's the liquor. Marks'll never rest till he's uprooted it. I'd best go on and carry it out, like I planned."

" 'Twould be wisest efn you left it lay. You 'n' me's got other business to tend. Micajah can lose that and no harm."

" 'Tain't 'Cajah's losing it, it's Marks' finding it that gramyes me," Ed said.

They got up and went carefully to the road again. And they stopped to listen, but Marks had long gone off. Still they went gently, until they were so far as Uncle Shannon Budd, who was yet sitting in his misery.

"Might 'a' been knowen," he jeered. "Fayre Jones sets out to rub a man down with a hickory stick, and comes on back neighborly as common. All you Gillows is that way."

Ed shut him up. "You're a sneap, you are. Get up offen that bank."

"Disabled to," Uncle Shannon said. "Whatever come over Joe Marks? He come pacing by and never so much as hailed a person. All tempered up, and left me set!"

Together they laid hold and straightened him out and balanced him in the road, though he called them fearsome names.

"Listen here," Fayre said, "gin you crave a drop o' freshening, Ed's got a piece o' news for you."

"Keep on toward Pilot," Ed told him, "and down at the fork of the branch, below a rock this end of the foot-log, you'll come on a bottle of the only medicine to cure rheumatism."

"Eh?"

"You heard me. Go on now. No call to act stiff in the joints."

They watched him to make sure he had right use of his knees again, while he tried out his steps.

"Reckon I can make it," he said directly.

"That's cheerfuller," Fayre said. "Hirple on, now!"

Uncle Shannon set forward. "Well for you," he called back through the darkness, "well for you that you got the rightful medicine handy, the way you tore me in pieces!"

He being gone, the threatening jower could not be put aside a further minute. It was nearly melted already with so much natural goings-on.

"I come out seeking you," Fayre said, as they tramped along.

"And found me," Ed owned.

"Efn I might work up a loathing," Fayre said, "I'd be glib to light into you. Trouble with me is I fail of a proper mislike. Seems I've not got it in head that you'd harm her or me either."

"O' course," Ed told him, "I got a fondness for

Bess Howard—who'd not have? But most likely when I run mad 'twill be after a sturdier piece."

"Hit's town's talk stirred me up," Fayre went on. "They said, 'There's Fayre Jones' pledged girl running wild; he'd ought to fight with some man.' And they kept frecking at me and pointing me out—me being known for a guardful man."

Working this matter out in slow words, Fayre saw a clear light. "Come to think," he said at last, "that's the way a heap o' quarrels is builded."

"That's how 'tis," Ed agreed, "a hardness grows betwixt neighbors and talk won't be content till it blossoms in a rippit."

"They called me nidget," Fayre said bitterly.

"Tell you what," Ed promised. "All is, I'll keep a shut mouth till No. 6 runs Monday morning and they'll be glib to make talk o' the way you run me out o' town."

"Time Uncle Shannon gets in, he'll spoil that lie."

"Didn't we this minute send him where he'll be disabled to talk of any matters till days along? Me, I'm due back at Massengale, and I'd not have come it, only you plucked me out of Marks' claws. You run me out o' town though I'd as leave you'd done it without driving my front teeth loose."

Fayre plodded on in a queer and joyful misery, wondering was he contented. "Seems like," he said, "I ain't the onliest one in Glen Hazard fails of craving a ruction."

"No call to tempt a person," Ed told him sharply. "First news and we'll be right at it."

"Only it pleasured me to be knowen we're yet cûd," Fayre said. "A good journey to you, and a light winter."

CHAPTER XIX

MIDDLEWARD of the week next following, Fayre made long steps to Micajah Dobbs' cave, and it was evening. The day went away with a deep white glow that comes after sun going down in still weather, and the blank sky was scrawled across with tree branches at its lower edge.

Fayre stopped and smelled at the losing day and shook a doubtful head.

"Tastes powerful dubersome," he said. "Come the cold yet fails, we're bound for wrack as easy as going down hill."

And he went on with a shudder between his shoulder blades that came over him such times as he had any matter to tend, and his hand was in his pocket with Micajah's bill, for he was set to be rid of this last thing that was cankering his mind.

The way was dark with sourwood and shingle oak grown close, and scuppernong vines were a snare to his feet, and sticky spider-webs caught across his face. Drifted leaves shushed under his tread, while he lagged through the slow miles and bethought him that always tomorrow is better than today for dangerous business.

And the nearer he dandered to Micajah's the more fearsome he was, until by such time as he came to the hole in the hillside, there was nothing but a picture of a smooth white headstone on a new grave, and the words:

HERE LIES
FAYRE JONES

And he came to the cave and cried out softly, thinking that did he call low, none might answer, and he would go away. But Dite Morgan came out.

"He's within," Dite told him, and would have gone his way, but Fayre bid him linger.

"There's a thing I crave you to witness to."

"I got more to do than nurse your affairs," Dite grumbled, but he went back with Fayre into the cave.

Micajah sat cross-legged in front of his still, seriously studying its yield, and in the unholy light he looked more than usually like a thing a person had thrown out. And his shadow was an unshapely heap on the rock wall.

Dite and Fayre sat them down.

Fayre was uneasied to begin speaking, and Micajah was a man that misliked to make first words, and it was none of Dite's affairs. So there was only the huffing of smoke in the chimney place, and far noises from the lost world outside. Minutes crawled by like flies till they were an hour and more thick. Then one of them buzzed into Micajah and startled him to words.

"No use to whimper 'n' fret about cash money, Fayre Jones," he said. "You'll not win ary other penny offen me. The road'll go on in spring just like always."

"I fail of craving talk of the road," Fayre said, while he watched the fire's flicker.

But Micajah made a sorrowful chant. "And this unwholesome winter's garred the men take out from here to far places. Times gets harder. I fail of being knowen wherefore the Lord should trouble me. I never meddled with Him."

Fayre pulled the fifty-dollar bill from his pocket and flung it in the fire. Dite Morgan reached for it and got burned fingers for his trouble; while Fayre wiped his hands up and down on his knees, cleaning off the touch of the money.

"You're knowen why I done that, Micajah Dobbs," he said.

Micajah went on with his chant: "And the road'll go on. Underneath the slipping clay there's rock. They'll make the road, and all will go on . . ."

"Hush that yatter!" Fayre said, and it was such long years since a person had dared speak harshly to Micajah that he stopped in a surprise.

"You shamed me," Fayre said. "You double shamed me, and I aim to break off with you and be a free man."

Dite Morgan leaned forward in a puzzle.

Fayre went on: "Me getting mixed with your trashy affairs was just me being weak-minded, and I never faulted you for that; only you double shamed me! First off you buy my tongue, and then you put me in a shameful place with Nels Ansen. Come I took up to his house, red-hot to pay him binding money, he only looked at it and give it back."

Dite was getting some sharp fun out of this talk, watching Micajah out of words, and Fayre Jones in the only fighting tantrum he'd been known to have. Dite's burned fingers leaned him to Fayre's side.

"What come?" he asked Fayre. "My wits is blind."

"What come!" Fayre cried out. "Nothing, only that bill was sham paper! Leave alone it's a sorry one who'd buy a man with sound money—think about 'Cajah here buying me with false money. My mind was that knock-kneed I took it, being gramyed with such need as overcome reason. Sham paper!"

Dite turned out all his pockets and took a sharp look at the balance of his last wages. It being good, he put it back, but this thing gave him a notion about using with Micajah Dobbs. "A person's scarcely safe risking the law all his days for maybe sham wages at the last," he growled to Fayre.

Micajah made no answer to what Fayre was saying, and Fayre left him there and went out a free man, and a bold one that had spoken out unafraid.

He climbed from the hidden path and set his face cleanly to the way before him. There was a light feel to the air, and he went along wondering if this was what happiness was. Folks talked about that, but Fayre had never met it until this minute.

The world was barren as ever of his needs, but it held a hope that he could take what he craved. Never again would he drift about waiting for other folk to order this or that. This life was his, and he went unbounden.

"There never was a man like me!" he cried out, making cheerful steps to Howard's Place. "There never was a man like me for picking up matters and walking forthrightly."

As he went up, he made a long story that he should tell Bess; and it was builded of all the fine things he dreamed, until by the time he was standing at the door there was no bolder man on earth. And, furthermore, he had stood up to Ed Gillow.

When he entered in the house, Homer said: "Blessed forever! efn here ain't Fayre Jones. Enter 'n' rest! Come here, Bess, here's a piece of news come walking in on two legs!"

And when she was come in, Fayre said: "You ain't forgot me, I hope?"

And she answered him: "I fail of thinking of only one person days in and out. I got a heap to do besides studying about which way your eyebrows is set, and how big your ugly mouth is, and why your nose turns up just that way; and the way you grip your hands times you get frecked over some matter; and the kind of swing to your walk gin you get mad at a person. No, sir, I got more in head than to be studying about that."

And she being the very inside of his heart, he

found himself disabled to tell a thing but the truth, and he poured out all the strife and bearm of the last days, ending up even by telling his fear of Micajah the way that shadow overhung him; and he told how there was no hope of more money from that corner of the world.

"As well," Bess said, "as well you got better sense than to come around this house with ary trace of that moldwarp to smirch you."

"Yet we're bad off as ever," he lamented. "Ansen fails of giving a sign; and I'm bound to take you—the way you're too dainty-looking to be left around to be ate up. Think about Ed, now!"

He said this roundly, so he might go on to tell her how he had becalled Ed over that affair, and he waited for her to say proud words over him.

But Bess said: "That wasn't but a play-game me and Ed fixed up."

And watching him go faded white, she saw—what any wiser woman might have told her—that there's a heap of facts in this life there's no need to pester a man by telling him.

"Nought but a play-game," he said slowly. "He likely was making mock of me that night—and me believing him friendly."

Bess wished her words back, but already she had cut his pride from under, and he was shamed past all curing.

"A pretty one you are to be faulting me!" he cried out. "And to shame me like that before all—making sport o' me with Ed Gillow. I reckon every man in town was knowen Ed not dangerous. I'd not be surprised did you tell each one your ownself."

When he started he had not seen how far he might run, but now Bess put her head in her arms and was crying against the table in quick choking gasps as if he had struck her.

"You've no call to go on that way, Bess," he said. " 'Twas only neat meanness of me—my mind never charged you with such—honest, it never."

And later he said: "Come I get Ansen's Place, we'll go away from here. A man and woman's got to live to theirselves. Folks like you 'n' me plain ain't skilled to dwell in towns."

Bess turned her head sideways on her arms and looked at him with one sad, wet blue eye.

"Efn you had a place *give* you, you'd lose it. You've not got the grasp. We'd both lose together."

"Hark to me!" Fayre said, in such a brand-new voice that Bess sat up to hear what. "There's many a one ain't the getting kind, but he does proudly with what's got. Some way I'll figure it yet, and it wouldn't surprise me didn't the Lord take pity and loan me a hand. And come he does so, I'm the man that'll stay in my natural place and work myself inside out to shelter you."

"I just see us now," Bess said miserably. "You and me walking barefooted up the railroad forever, seeking a homeplace. You 'n' me, just begging through life forever and ever."

"Well," Fayre said, perfectly like a man, "so long as it was me *and* you . . ."

"O, Land o' Souls!" Bess cried out, jumping up. "Get out o' here. I've seen enough of you to do me a year and more."

"THERE never was a man like me," Fayre lamented as he tramped to his lonely shed. "There never was a man like me for landing back where he started. My life goes around in rings. Hit's no surprise I get took with dizzy spells."

CHAPTER XX

THE threat of the late fall was fulfilled, and there was wretchedness in Glen Hazard and in all the country that lay round about. The end of the year drew near and there was yet no sign of winter. The unforgiving sun festered the swamp places, drank up the streams and burned last sap from growing things; and when a warm rain came and ended in fog, instead of a wholesome coldness, the townsmen knew that deadly times were come upon them and were afraid. The sickness came first in the valley places, and crept up surely from the coves, and low fever took the mountain townships one by one.

In Glen Hazard the weekdays were quiet as Sunday, for the big mill and the hardwood factory were closed down, and there was no more neighboring in Gillow's Store. Those who came took up their goods and hastened away, asking rare questions and fearing the answers. For a neighbor would go out from town to his far homeplace and being not come again in the week thereafter, one would say: "We

"I got to go on," Fayre said, standing uneasily by the door.

Aunt Matt came to herself on the instant.

"Dummered efn I ain't acting like the only person left on earth!" she cried, while she jumped up. "Set you down, Fayre Jones, whilst I fix you up a dose of coffee and spice cookies. You're all dragged out, and me with not the sense to hearten you. Tell your news."

"Not doing much good," Fayre told her, as he settled into a chair again, "but yet able to be here and there."

"Poor folks got to say 'kind thanks' for little these times. Heard where Doc's using Bess heavily and finding out she's a handy nurse."

Fayre made no words till he had swallowed his coffee in one long drink.

"Surely freshens a man," he said, "and I thank you greatly. Scarcely I see her. Times I go up to Homer's she's gone off to be a help where need is, and gin we do chance, there's scant words."

Aunt Matt gathered to her sewing work again, and made speed for the time she'd lost, while her tongue matched her needle.

"Waits Lowe's everywhere about," she said. "Sam come back from store and tells where Ranson Gillow's books never will be right again, the way that boy's addling around. Seems Waits'll walk in and gather up goods and go off with 'em, and only fling back over his shoulder, 'Put it down to Barts' or whoever. Or maybe he'll say, 'Them Morgans got to have meal and disabled to pay—set it down on my bill or Rashe's.' Sam tells where Ranson'll be struggling in the Post Office corner with a heap of unfetched mail and grunts out 'Yes' and forgets who."

Aunt Matt took breath, and Fayre, being pleasured to hear her like commonly again, said: "Waits is surely the carriest person, fetching food and water to a sight o' houses, and turning out o' doors such as Doc's ordered in the air. Happen I'll go in and speak with Morris?"

"Gin he's wakeful," Aunt Matt said, "only watch you'll not freck him."

In the next minutes Fayre came solemnly out from Morris's room.

"Believe I'll set out."

"Hit *does* seem like the Lord neglects us," Aunt Matt said.

A sky the color of ashes lay close above the earth, and the air hung breathless in the tangled trees. Time was dead and all sorrow had come home, and the world was far past Fayre's understanding. When he came to the steep above Glen Hazard he waited to look down upon it. The little town lay crushed and gray and very bleak, and only scant smoke struggling from its chimneys showed there was yet some living going on there. Days had gone by on heavy feet and tramped its heart out, and now there was only so much rain as served to make the streets a grease to walk in, and at the last of the outworn year the days trod wanly through winter leaving muddy tracks.

Fayre was taken with a great loneliness, and a craving to strip back this gray weight of sorrow with his big, willing hands, and see if happen the town might not come bright again like former times. And in the midst of such useless notions, he came on Waits Lowe, bound in his same path.

"Tell how Morris goes on," Waits asked.

"He's poorly. Happen you can tell where Doc has ordered Bess? She'll be took down with all this."

They held the road together so far as town.

"Reckon Morris being weak from his hurt leg is

what garred him took the fever so hard. No, I've not seen Bess in long ever."

"Be a joyous day when all's overpast," Fayre said.

Waits was saddened. "Liable to be none left to rejoice."

"Doc Peters and the Lord'll save a remnant between 'em."

"For a nervous man like you, you fail of caring for your skin," Waits said. "I heard tell where you . . ."

"There's sense 'n' reason to helping sick folks," Fayre said quickly.

Waits shook a worried head. "My stomach gars me turn flinch. Hit's powerful skittish. A open fight's one thing—but this sickness that gars a man die, trapped in his house, like maybe a rat—phah!"

"Likely we'd be in a worse state, but only for Doc Peters," Fayre went on directly.

"Doc ain't so much," Waits said. "He's a good man and a busy one, yet times I misdoubt me he fails of being knowen what best to do."

"Give no more hard words about him," Fayre warned. "One more, and I'll ding you foolish in the head."

And Waits laughed to see the easy-hearted Fayre

so tempered, and only to plague him he said: "Who may you think yourself to order a man like me? Doc's *ordinary!*"

And then he was looking up at Fayre, whose face danced over above him all mixed with sparks of light; and Fayre reached down a hand and yanked Waits to his feet saying: "What come over me is unknowen!"

The blood had drained down from Fayre's face and the glow was all gone out of him. They stood in the midst of the gray fog and Waits had a sharp hurt in his eye that felt big as an apple; and Fayre looked at the place on his hand where it was skinned, and he said: "I'm took aback at my ownself!"

"That's what being friends is," Waits mocked him. "Happen knocking a man down over a careless word is the neighborlest thing to do!"

"Doc's a friend o' mine," Fayre said.

"Keep him," Waits answered, "but I'll not be laid waste gin you feel edgy." And he went on his way, dabbing a handkerchief to his eye, and Fayre was in great misery.

Fayre searched through Glen Hazard for the house where Bess might be. They saw each other scantly during the sadded days, going in and out of one house or another, stopping on errands to ask news, and in these swift, unkind minutes they feared and their hearts were weighted. But they gave each other over to the common needs.

He came upon her directly furthermost the tracks and making her way homeward.

There was not much of Bess in her sturdiest times and she was more pinched with each passing day; her eyes were heavy and her face white. Fayre himself was only walking bones with tired eyes deep in his head.

"Have a care for yourself!" Fayre greeted.

"And you," she said quietly. Her thoughts were prisoned far away looking for the end of sadness.

"Morris Ott's low. Seems being weak from lying up this summer, he's disabled to gainstand it."

" 'Tis a grief for Aunt Matt and others."

"There's a change come over Morris. Up there this evening, I asked him didn't he fret to be doing around like he used, and he only said, 'I crave my life, but not so well I'd not be content to lose it.' I made sport of him, trying might I stir him up, but he only said, 'Desire's melted in me.' And Aunt Matt said not to pester him."

"What ails your hand?"

"Me 'n' Waits chipped out a while back. 'Tain't nothing."

"Come up house and leave me wrap it."

"Surely no; 'tain't nothing. I'll be on my way. A safe night to us all!"

Bess watched him go, and being utterly wearied out, she thought about the thankful times, when she might be tending her own house and Fayre would be coming home each night and she could wrap his hurts if so minded. And about them calling him flinch! Then she recalled that the thankful times might never come, and gave over watching him, and climbed the homeward path with cumbered feet.

CHAPTER XXI

On an early morning when the clouds yet strangled the hopeless trees, Virgil Howard came riding through the dark woods too tired to hear a thing save the sucking clop of his horse's tread on the soft trail. The Preacher had gone so lank and worn that, going through the blackness of the forest on his tall white horse, he might have been taken for a ghost already. His ministry had been a heavy one in the past weeks, for he had prayed heart into many a home that had nearly given over; but some had turned from him, saying he was overly full of cheerfulness to save souls out of a perishing world. And truly he had seen sights that stretched his own faith to the point of wondering what the Lord might be thinking of.

Where the Red Hill road joins the low trail that surrounds Cragg, he came on Rashe Lowe, making toward Glen Hazard at a laggard's pace.

"You're puffing like you walked a far piece

a'ready," the Preacher greeted him, whilc he climbed down from his horse to walk beside.

"Used to be I owned the proudest legs in all these hereabouts," Rashe complained, "and now, time I got most use for 'em, in these days of fetch-'n'-carry, they start to fail me. I been bedfast a full-sized week with their achements."

" 'Tis evil days, truly," Virgil said; and he stopped to turn his horse loose, the way he had no need of him in town.

"They fare poorly over to Four Mile," Rashe said. "I hear where they've got 'em a town-fetched doctor-person. Thank mercies we're not come to that pass yet."

"Liable to, gin Peters fails of his strength. He's mightily downgone."

"And, do his mightiest," Rashe agreed, "he's disabled amongst the spaced-out homesteads. I seen where some o' the folk in lone places is using old-time remedies, and some even took to charms and witching."

Fayre Jones came pouring by them, and when he saw who was, he pulled up and went alongside.

"Efn here ain't Doc's shadow his ownself!" Rashe said. "Tell news."

"News ain't fitten, only there's been a mucker back Wild Cat way, due to 'Cajah Dobbs working up a deadly brew outen a old charm book; and he 'n' Dite drank at it till they failed of telling night from day. Lay stupid a week or more."

"Happen you run on 'Cajah's behalf—he being a famous friend to you?" Rashe asked directly, while he swung along to keep pace until they were come girt Cragg Hill westerly.

Fayre tramped his way to more words: "No more had Doc threatened they'd be dead, than here come 'Cajah, hirpling 'round brisk as a dewberry, and having the magic to sell. That's how it come to pass that Uncle Shannon Budd was altogether spoiled by drinking Micajah's cure. I take a turn here," he ended, and was gone along a thwart path.

"Hi!" Virgil Howard called him, "you neglected to say was he safe dead?"

Fayre cried back over his shoulder: "Nuh-uh! Doc Peters brought him alive again by hard measures."

"We be two old men," Rashe said, while they stood to rest before they should take the last down slant.

"Each of us ripe for our end," Virgil agreed.

"A man's got to go some day or another."

They waited side by side, drawing courage each from the other.

"Times like this, years make no matter. There's Ranson Gillow's youngest, took sick day afore yesterday and gone a'ready. Went like a plucked flower-thing."

"Better have been me," Virgil growled.

"Or me . . ."

"You!" Virgil whirled about and shouted at his old friend with snapping eyes. "You, that's gnarledy as a oak and strong as a millwheel!"

"Reckon a millwheel ever gets weak trembles in its legs?" Rashe answered seriously.

" 'Tis a heart-searching time," Virgil said, as they went down. "Seems most folk commonly given to church-going have forgot to pray, and spend a power o' time quarreling at the Lord, whilst a mort o' hard-swearing sinners is turned staunch and helping."

Rashe said: "Only scant weeks gone, Waits was telling where Fayre Jones played in Gillow's field, fellowly with them younglings."

Doc Peters was struggling along the crest of

Coal Hill easterly and while he came down aslant, Virgil and Rashe came in from their side, and the three met in town's center, barren of all save themselves.

The doctor was bent-shouldered, and not so fat as in former times, and he was wearied out till he had no more go in him than an unwound clock.

"Give you good cheer, Peters!" the Preacher greeted.

But the doctor returned him a dour look. "Time has gone by for your cheer treatment," he said. "Good words are no way useful when a whole people is laid low."

Virgil's fighting chin came forward.

"All is, Peters," he said, "a fearful folk is woeful hard to guide, and more times than once I've heartened 'em to bestir and do as you ordered."

"They'd do it sharp enough without you under foot," the doctor answered. "I never did favor religion. Liable to weaken a man—though I got to own it has not harmed you 'specially."

Virgil began: " 'Tis the visitation of the Lord. . . ."

" 'Tis nothing of the kind," the doctor said,

while he sat down to rest on the stone foot of the water tower. " 'Tis the visitation of slacktwistedness. When times come that folk clean up their properties or ever they sit down to study the Scriptures, we'll be spared a power of such 'visitations.' "

"Same thing," Virgil said peacefully, "only way the Lord's got to learn humans is to leave 'em get embrangled. Like our young-uns. We tell 'em our wiseness, and they make no matter of it. They got to find out by getting hurt. They've a rather for it."

"That's how come the world don't get on faster, I'd not be surprised," Rashe said. "But Doc's got reason. A power o' caddle is made by folks that undertake to be holy whilst they leave matters go to wrack. How soon do you reckon these times'll be overpast?"

"It would be a hard saying," Doc Peters answered, while he hoisted himself from the block. "The set of the sky gives no promise. Better let the Preacher go pray for a hard freeze."

Virgil looked at this man, who worked days long and most nights also, practising righteousness, yet claimed he believed nothing whatever. Doc Peters' face was gray and his eyes hard and swollen from lack of sleep, but his mouth was twisted into a grin as he made sport of the Preacher.

"Saving I'm knowen of your good works," Virgil said severely, "I'd gar you cease making mock. As 'tis, I'll lay it up to used-outness. Likely the Lord's long since done the same."

The doctor made off. "Give you good-day," he said.

But Rashe Lowe stopped him. "Now that I got you two within a arm's length," he said, laying a hand on Virgil Howard, who was backing off, "I mean to see you neighborly. Hit's beyond all reason, you old men acting tutly. There's room in this town for a Preacher and a Doctor both, I trust?"

"Howard and me never did set our minds to agree together," Doc said.

"And where's the need of that?" Rashe asked. " 'Twould be a dull world did all think one thing."

"Well," Doc agreed, "so he keeps his prayers out of where I'm busy, he's welcome to exhort when I'm gone the house."

Virgil said: "All is, we're all of us threadbare with this winter's happenings, and temper speaks out where reason is dried up."

They looked upon one another long and seriously; and between them there was fellowship, only never would they own so much in flat-out words.

And when Doc Peters went off across town, Rashe and Virgil watched him go, and Virgil said: "He's not good my way, but I'd not be surprised didn't the Lord find him mighty useful odd times."

And Rashe answered: "Heap o' folks is good enough for the Lord that fails of being good enough for each other. I'm broguing up to Homer's. He's perfectly misput with nothing to do but look out of the window and count how the hours go by."

CHAPTER XXII

BACK in Sam Ewart's house Morris Ott lay quiet and watched the last shadows gather. His bed was in the middle of the room to get such air as might be stirring, and the door and window both stood wide, for he kept crying out for air, though all that came was thick and wet with fog.

From the mill yard came the noise of hammering, for Sam Ewart no more sat on a log and planned how he might get rich. He made coffins and sold them for the price of the wood only, since it was not to his liking to gain money in such manner.

"Night comes soon," Morris whispered.

Aunt Matt pulled the curtains back and sought for the day's last light, but gray, short days are merciless in the land of many shadows.

"A man rides up from town," she told Morris, "but I'm disabled to make him out."

She went to the fire and stacked it up freshly, but it could not burn. It choked and blinked, and the thick blue smoke dragged itself slowly from around the logs.

"Time to quit work," Morris said, so low that Aunt Matt scarcely heard.

"Sam'll quit right away now; hit's darkling so he'll not see his way. That noise uneasies me."

"Me, too. Who comes?"

"That's Preacher Howard's tone," Aunt Matt said. "I'll go cry him in. Sam's given over his racket, thank mercies!"

When she was gone, the room was still—so quiet in the last evening that Morris was aware how still himself lay; and he heard the roughness of his cold hands on the blanket. The room smelled of yellow soap and drifted wood-smoke.

Voices came from the yard, mixed all together, louder as they neared the house, Virgil telling news in the same gentle thunder of a church talk, and Sam's high shout breaking in with questions, and then in a quiet space Aunt Matt urging: "Step in 'n' see him."

They were in the kitchen. And Morris, suddenly afraid in the dark, called them to come in, but they went on with their talk, unhearing. And he tried to call louder and started a cough that brought Aunt Matt running.

She tucked in the bedding and put his hands beneath the covers, and while she brisked around she scolded: "Keep under there, for patience' sake, you're cold as cold. Little more 'n' I'll shut the window on you! You wait till I tell Doc Peters—the way you act!"

He lay quiet. "I declare, he's asleep a'ready." She stopped and bent her head close to his. "Morris Ott, you quit acting up!"

He opened his eyes that no more looked eagerly for what might happen.

"Hot!" he whispered.

He was burning hot—all but his feet; they were cold as if he were standing in a spring freshet. There were other boys wading in the stream, little fellows around ten years old, and over above them was Dilla Ott, the woman who had raised him with her six boys; and she called out: "Come out o' that—quick now!" And they all stayed and were ashamed to come out, since she would flog them for being in cold water too soon in the year; also they were naked.

"I'll go after Doc my ownself!" Dilla cried out; but it was Aunt Matt's voice.

The other boys were gone away, all but Dite Morgan. How had he come there? And he had a rope that he threw around Morris to drag him up among the bushes. It caught him around the throat, so he strained and twisted.

"He said he'd come this way up tonight, but you'd best hasten him, the way he looks." The voice cut sharply into the darkening room.

Morris choked and writhed and could not cry out. Then hands were laid on him, and he looked up to see Preacher Howard, as he was forced down full length into the icy water. He gasped and shuddered against the cold sheet.

And night being fully come, Morris lay at peace, his short days mercifully fulfilled.

SAM and Aunt Matt being come to the door of the room, waited there, and Virgil Howard came out to them and closed the door softly.

"The world can't give him a thing more," Virgil said.

They were all three in the kitchen place, and

they stood around the stove until the grateful fire had warmed their first chill.

The men sat down and Aunt Matt moved quickly to carry a candle to the inner room and shut the window there. She came back and set the kettle of water forward on the stove.

When they heard Doc Peters, Sam opened the outer door, and he came and sat with them.

Aunt Matt said: "His eyes and his heart both are quiet."

And Sam spoke fiercely: "I'll not build a coffin for him!" As if, should he hold out, this might bring Morris back.

Doc Peters looked in the red glow of the fire-box a long while, and he said bitterly: "And our years come and come and come!"

"Leave him go where a man may bare his soul," Virgil said. "Our turn comes fairly when our use is done."

Aunt Matt twisted her handkerchief round and round her work-rough fingers, while she said: " 'Tis a piteous thing for one so young and wistly to be in a narrow grave. And his eyes were always seeking. . . ."

Virgil Howard said: "And his seeking will be comforted."

Darkness of the room was heavy upon them, and wavering fire showed through the stove's cracks, and unreal shadows felt for steady hold upon the walls.

Doc Peters spoke on a sudden: "We got no proof o' that!"

"Faith's a sturdier thing," Virgil answered him. "Hit ain't so liable to slip up and meet accidents, the way proofs do. Faith's a proud thing and we all die by it."

"How come we do? What goes with those of us that fail of having it?"

"You also. Bound to, at the last, since there's naught else to have." The Preacher stood up straight, and his shadow filled all the kitchen place. "There's ne'er a proof made that can stand in the presence of the dying," he said. "Only the living may lean on such signs."

Doc Peters shook his head. "Maybe I'll not find my way so clear as you, Virgil Howard, but you're most strangely common for a Lord's man."

And he went into the inner room, and when he was come out he and the Preacher left the house that they might be company one for the other so far as the town.

CHAPTER XXIII

THE graveyard on Big Gully Hill was the brightest place in all the sorry land. Yellow clay and red clay of the many new-turned mounds gleamed brightly among the pent roofs of tar paper that shield the edge graves from washing down the slope, and in the far corners the evergreen vines grew tangled over long-lost mounds of former years. Under the ghostly sky this burial ground lay strangely bright with the false flowers the women had contrived from colored paper—these being all they had to offer.

Bess Howard put her arms around Aunt Matt Ewart, where they stood by the latest grave of all, and back of them were voices speaking good things that were remembered of Morris Ott. And she looked across to where the men were standing, leaning on their shovels and waiting each for the other to move off. Fayre Jones was watching Preacher Howard, who was at the grave's head and the Preacher's last words came firmly— ". . . and here we leave him resting beyond this world's harshness; and there shall be no more grief, if only we take our religion the way the Lord meant us to take it."

"We may as well go down," Aunt Matt said at last.

And the hantle of neighbors drifted slowly away. Bess and Aunt Matt went last and Sam Ewart and Fayre Jones with them. So they walked back from Big Gully graveyard toward Glen Hazard, over the road most used in the last hard weeks. And at the foot of Cragg Hill they took their several ways, and went each to his own house.

BACK in her own place, Aunt Matt stood at the door of the inner room. And there was only the gleam of the smooth white counterpane where the bed was lone among the grayness.

"I declare," Aunt Matt said, "some way ought to be figured so a person's leftments would vanish away. Hit's the terriblest thing to paw over things that's no more use. Makes a person feel like a needle-nose worthless."

She went in and began to take clothing from the

corner shelves and odd boxes from the fireboard. But there was no heart in her for such work.

Sam came to the doorway to see what her grumbling was about. "Hit's a job to be done," he said, "and a hard task don't get softer with leaving it lay."

"For track's sake, Sam, go someplace else to be wise," Aunt Matt said.

She emptied a suitcase and some boxes on the bed and turned out the pockets of spare clothing ere she folded it to one side. There were only common things—a pencil stub, and a comb, and a frayed letter with a list on the back of it of stuff he'd meant to buy down at Gillow's. Only the next day he had broken his leg. Must have been back in August he wrote that. Aunt Matt threw it down with things to burn.

Then there was a picture of a hantle of schoolchildren; must have been taken years gone, for there was Fayre and Ed and Bonnie Gillow and Morris himself. Aunt Matt lighted the lamp the better to see it. They were standing in long rows, and Bess Howard was a middle one. Morris had drawn an ink ring around her head, so the picture was just Bess for him—all the picture he had of her. Aunt Matt threw it down to burn, saying: "Shucks! there's no more use to it now." And picked it up again saying: "Still 'n' all . . ." And kept it a long while in her hand, while time slid away.

And when she could make no move against such things, she went back to the clothes, for they could be set aside more readily. But when she came to more papers in an overcoat pocket, she craved help. Aunt Matt knew lawyers' papers by sight, and they gave her chills, since they always spelled signing away one house and taking up another. Here was such a one now, narrow and white, with printing on the back.

She called Sam. "Go you down and gather Sheriff Marks and Ranson Gillow, so's we may deal rightly with these papers."

Sam grumbled: "Tomorrow morning would be handier. Day grows late."

"You grow worthless," she said. "Let's get this business over with, so's Morris can rest quiet."

So they were gathered about the table in the kitchen place that same night, with the lamp in the midst and their faces shadowed. And Virgil Howard also was with them, being stopped on his way by Sam, when he fetched Marks and Gillow. And soon, while they were yet waiting each for the other to speak, came a cry at the gate and Uncle Shannon Budd entered with them, he having smelled news.

"I set out same time as you, Virge Howard," he panted, "but was disabled to keep up with that horse you ride on. He's got more legs than me—'tain't fair."

Uncle Shannon was no matter, but they scarce could turn him forth, so they bid him to a chair by the stove, and looked once more at the papers.

Sam said: "Matt and me come to nothing of much use, but there's a heap of small matters for whosoever heirs to Morris Ott's things; especially does this paper read like I made out. That's property, that paper is, and what kin has Morris got?"

Sheriff Marks unfolded the paper. "Hit's a straight deed," he said. "Properties down Grassy Cove. How come he by that, d'you reckon?"

"Likely on some trade," Virgil said, "but where's it to go to?"

" 'Course," Aunt Matt said, "Morris was a Gillow, one of Lake's—your own brother's, Ranson. You recollect how them young-uns was neighbored out after Brutus Morgan killed Lake."

Ranson nodded. "I failed of keeping track," he said. "Being I was disabled to do for 'em my ownself, I was kind of 'shamed to follow 'em out. I recall Morris was raised by the Otts, but he was one of Lake's boys, doubtless, and Fayre . . ."

"There's no question of Ott being a Gillow," Virgil said. "Now we got to find is there more of Lake's children so's to see who comes by this property. I disremember what come to 'em."

Ranson Gillow started to speak, but Uncle Shannon, who had already taken a sound sleep, came awake on a sudden, and shouted from his dark corner: "Properties!"

This gave no help to the affair and Uncle Shannon went to sleep again unthanked.

"Seems Bess Howard ought to heir, since it'd be what Morris wanted done," Aunt Matt said. "But o' course, she's no kin."

Ranson went on: "And Fayre Jones, he's one of the Gillows."

"Love us all!" Aunt Matt cried out, "that'd make you own uncle to Fayre!"

"Supposing it does," Ranson said, "I ain't ashamed of him."

Sheriff Marks charged him, saying: "How come you concealed this fact?"

"Hit never come up till this minute," Ranson told him sharply. "I ain't no long-mouth. None asked me. Soon's ever you read the deed, I spoke out fast as I could, only some others had to keep putting in."

Virgil said: "Must be I'm getting old. I was knowen Fayre's folks was Gillows and never put the two notions together. Dull, that's what I am."

Uncle Shannon said from his corner: "Virge Howard's dull." And when none took notice of him, he only said: "But, Lord help us, most of us *is* dull."

Sheriff Marks said: "Then, judgmatically, there's only Fayre Jones."

"Fayre Jones ain't dull," Uncle Shannon quarreled. "Nice boy, Fayre Jones. A helpsome boy. Picks up a man's rheumatism, him 'n' Ed, and gives good blockade to heal him."

"That's how it was and where it went!" the Sheriff said. "You go on back to sleep, you old trash heap."

But Uncle Shannon was come broad awake, and rambled so far as the table.

"That paper's properties!" he said, while he took it up with his grimy hand. "Never owned but one such in all my days, and it got away from me, and here 'tis!"

Marks took it from him. "Leave it drap," he said, "the world's full of such papers."

"You give me my deed!" Uncle Shannon cried out. "I rapped it offen a man at Grassy Cove in a trade for a mule."

"Grassy Cove? You made up that lie this minute."

"I never! Ask Ranson! I recall me now, I give it to him and never lost it like I said."

"Give it here," Ranson said. "One time this old clutch-fist did swap me a land deed for five years' back store-goods. Maybe he fails of lying this once."

Sam Ewart said: "For mercy sake, Matt, set *down;* you'll have the lamp over next news!"

Ranson held the deed close to the light, but there was nothing to see but a gray patch where pencil writing had been smudged. The Sheriff bumped his head against Ranson's.

"There's been endorsements there one time," he said.

Ranson ended up: " 'Tis the same deed Uncle Shannon give me, and I made it over to . . ." He stopped. "Me and Micajah Dobbs had a trade over . . . I disrecall, but we had a trade, and he took this."

He turned his head slowly and looked at the Sheriff, who stared back at him, each waiting for the next word. At last they straightened up.

Marks said: "Hit's this deed we're talking of, and Wild Cat's out o' my territory anyway."

"That's how come 'Cajah got it, and likely give it to Morris for wages."

"My head's got to going 'round," Sam Ewart said. "Looks like given time every person would have had it. Where's the sense each paying every with a deed to land none ever seen or valued? Happen it'd have come to me next, for Morris's board and keep, and I might have put me up a mill on it and got rich."

"Clear enough it come to Morris and clear that Fayre's heired to it rightfully," Marks said. "Reckon I'll be going on."

"Leave me company with you," Uncle Shannon said dolefully. "I been robbed, but seeing it's to go to Fayre Jones I'll not gainstand it. Fayre's a helpsome boy."

Aunt Matt was cheerfuller than she had been in long days and Sam called her down sharply for acting chipper at the wrong time.

"Likely it don't mean a thing to you menfolk," she said, "but Morris was heartsome to Bess and would be mainly proud she had a homeplace through him. She and Fayre can live down to Grassy Cove and . . ."

"Matt!" Sam told her. "Your tongue is unseemly. Still yourself!"

To pleasure Aunt Matt, the men left her to tell Fayre about his being brother to Morris Ott, and she sent word to him to come up house. And he came the next early morning, and Waitstill Lowe with him.

Aunt Matt was in the yard all in the midst of steam from the washtub, and while she soused the clothing, she edzacted it all out to them, and Fayre was struck wordless.

"Seems it don't mean a thing to you," Aunt Matt said, when he had sat still for a drearisome time—for she had looked for him to rejoice.

"He fails of taking it in yet," Waits excused him, "having him a homeplace so sudden-like gets bettermost of him."

"Bess'll never content herself to live down Grassy Cove," Fayre said dully.

"Pity you for a noggen!" Waits told him. "Ansen'll trade you. 'Tis the very place you talked of that day far back."

"Reckon I might?" Fayre said; and then: "Hit fails of pleasuring me much to heir a homeplace offen a dead man. Kind o' takes the spice out of it."

"Oh, great forever!" Waits said. "All this work you make over a homeplace, and come its handed to you on a platter, you've not got the up-'n'-at-it to grab hold. 'Tain't like it would fetch Morris back for you to leave it waste."

Aunt Matt broke in: "Never did hear tell of such a mix. Love 'n' sorrow walk hand in hand. Hit does seem you can't have one without the other."

She was standing over the wash-kettle seeing that the fire took a brisk, and on a sudden she made a motion of her hands as if she threw all troubles into the blaze. Her face was more at peace after that, and she stirred the fire with a long stick to be sure all was burned up.

"I never craved Morris should die," Fayre lamented.

"No more any of us," Waits answered, "but there's no help for that. Aunt Matt, see can you work some sense in this Seek-Sorrow. I'm all out o' patience."

And he took himself stamping out of the yard since he was no more use, and slammed the gate after him.

Aunt Matt went on talking while she rinsed and wrung and hung out. And she told how deeply Morris had craved after Bess for his own, and laid down to Fayre that it would pleasure Morris did Bess have a homeplace of his giving, till at last Fayre was content, and took himself homeward.

But there were yet clouds in the sky, and the going was solemn. And when the clouds broke and let through a trickle of sun, Fayre Jones lifted back his shoulders and cried out to the brightening day.

"I got me a family!" he chanted. "I'm a person that's sib with these parts—Lake Gillow's my father, and Morris my brother, and Ed my cousin—and I——got——folks!"

The clouds shut in once more, and a threatsome wind stirred the trees, and Fayre gave over his song and raced back to town out of the weather that was beginning to happen.

CHAPTER XXIV

THE wind grew like the roll of drums in the tree tops. In a sudden hour it came, throbbing and beating its way around the knees of those hills that sheltered the town. It jumped and raced and whirled in town's center, sending trash paper as high in the air as the water tank, and choking any who ventured withoutdoors.

All night it blew sturdy and roaring, and in the morning it was such a wind as might blow the world away. The sky was black with tumbling clouds that had no time to shed their rain and snow. The wind chased them, and hurled them over and over, and shrieked in temper when they failed of going fast enough.

Citizens lay crouched withindoors and housemates looked strangely upon one another, for the world was full of a terrible noise and the town trembled.

The higher houses clung bravely to the hillsides, but porch posts and pieces of roofing and whole sets of doorsteps let go and came hurtling down into the town. The railroad track was all distressed with scourings that fell from the easterly side, and every train that went by handily made kindling out of the trash.

Directly the wind was flecked with rain, for the over-heavy clouds first began to leak and drip; and the wind hurried on, leaving them to empty over Glen Hazard in a pelting onding.

Once the rain began it had no sense to leave off. It came down in a cold gray curtain for the three following days, and beat so hard that it jumped back off the earth until it was raining upwards and downwards both, and in the town it sprayed out from walls and roofs besides.

The streets were no better than creeks, and the water tower stood ankle deep in a swirl of yellow swash. Little North Fork so far forgot its manners that it climbed both banks and spread itself abroad in the Company's Store, and then went on down the road and drowned the machines at the big mill.

Being weather-trapped at Doc Peters' house, Fayre Jones mosed around and around the rooms like a pent possum, only being still such times as he pressed his face to the window pane.

"Gin this keeps on, Ansen's Place'll wash under ever I get to trade it," he fretted.

"A man can anyway rest his bones and not feel a stiving worthless," Doc Peters put in from the couch where he spent these useless days catching up with his fled sleep. "Such cleansing is wholesome, even supposing it is nervous weather."

"Happen I might climb so far as to visit with Bess 'n' Homer?" Fayre wondered directly. "Hit's a denial only going around and around."

"Should you set down and keep right still," the doctor said lazily, while the wind kicked the house so it shuddered, "gin this keeps on, Homer's house and all in it will be visiting on this roof and save you the steps."

But Fayre watched the drenching hours go by, restless for the time to come when he might go to Ansen's for he feared it would be altogether ruined. And at the first switch of the tempest's abating, he was out of the house, making excuse to Doc that they lacked meal and coffee and he was bound to go after it.

The clouds yet dripped, and Fayre drove himself forward against this misguided plash, and felt creepish at being abroad in such shameful wetness. And he saw many happenings that had gone on that made him fearful for his own place.

In the low farms the fields had gone under, stock was drowned in the sheds and fences melting down were floating off stick by stick. The road out to Newt Beechy's place was a river, and his barn that had been leaning aslant the road since a cross-prop fell out the forerunning summer had now been blown across it like a bridge. So flat it was, a wagon team might have been driven over it.

When Fayre got up so far as Ansen's, he cried the house and being hailed within he found Ansen tempting a wet wood fire to burn by sprinkling sugar on it. And this so used up his mind that he made no matter of Fayre, who waited while his sodden clothes made a pond on the floor that directly streamed across beneath Ansen's feet.

Ansen looked up.

"Det regnar," he said.

"Surely undoubtedly it does," Fayre answered, "and I took a fisherman's walk all the way up here to talk about trading what's left of this downgone place for a better."

ANSEN made no stir about the trade with Fayre.

And when the weather came to its right mind again, he went down to measure the properties with great care, and when Fayre next came back upon a reasonable day, Ansen only said: "Ja," and he flung his house things into his wagon, hitched the horse, tied the cow on behind and walked away without a farewell or a look backward.

Fayre stood on the porch, with a sharp and anxious face peering out between the collar flaps of his overcoat, looking at the stricken high fields and the drowned low places and the raw weather-painted buildings. And he wondered him what kind of a noggen he was to have made such work to possess this worthless place.

The iron-hard freeze had come after long days, and held all in a grip that seemed bent never to let go. Even the trash leavings of Ansen's move —old empty cans, a broken chair-leg and a halter strap—were frozen to the ground forever.

The coldness ate into Fayre till he turned withindoors, but this was no better. It was only three bare rooms, moved out of, and much litter spread around. The hole in the brick flue, where the stove had been, whistled to keep itself company, and a can, half full of green oil, alone on the window ledge, was the only furnishing. The house cracked and squeaked as Fayre trod the sunken floor boards; and it smelled of Ansen and his foreign cooking.

Truly he had gotten his homeplace, and a fit one to bring Bess Howard into!

Fayre came out again and pulled shut the reluctant door and, savagely, to prove it his own door, he turned the key and put it with sad pride in his pocket.

It was altogether the wrong time of year for homemaking, and Fayre saw why it was that weddings are commonly made in the springtime when all the world is brave with sun and flowers, and the first winter too far ahead for notice.

He set forth on heavy feet to go to Howard's, but when he came around the foot of Cragg Hill, he went up and across to Lowe's, for a man might get hold of himself with a friendly warm fire. Now that all was done and all he had to offer Bess was nothing worth, he was in need of heartening. So he came to Lowe's cabin, the little log house that had stood since the grandsir's grandsir had builded it.

CHAPTER XXV

At the end of the day, before an eager fire, past troubles ride light, and Fayre was more than half way come to himself again before any word was spoken. And in the first words Barsha Lowe took life by the hand and walked off with it.

She looked up from her patching work, and sniffed the warm air. "Beans for supper," she said, "and pickled peaches, and the coffee will be hot."

And when this good news had time to warm its way, she went on: "That's a thing that contents me with Dena. She has the coffee hot on cold nights. Looks like she might have been *born* a Lowe."

"She makes a good shape at a second-hand one," Waits said, while he brogued out to the kitchen-place to see what help he might be. And he left them in peace, which is what Barsha had counted on.

"The place ain't fitten," Fayre said.

"Likely not this night. Look at you—perfectly like all men—nothing in stomach, nothing in head."

She raised her voice and called to know were the beans cooked yet.

"No, they ain't, Needle-Nose," Waits called back. "They'll be all of five minutes."

"Hark to what you raised," Rashe growled from his corner. "Times I was a boy and called my folks out of name . . ."

"Your son also," Barsha answered him, "and I did cleverly to raise him at all, with you being a model all over the house."

Fayre lifted up his head and said on a sudden: "There's three rooms."

"Good news," Barsha said, "what more?"

Fayre held forth about Ansen's Place, all he could recall to its promise, and Barsha and Rashe gave willing ears, as if they had not been hearing the same story since long along.

Rashe said sternly: "Harness your pride, boy! Time I was a young-un, gin I'd had three rooms and all that land, the world wouldn't have held me."

"Pity the world!" Barsha said, "and my memory goes back that you were high-stomached enough over this place."

"What ails this place?"

"This place," Barsha said, after looking all

around it with a careful eye, "this place would have had more room in it efn it had been bigger."

Rashe kicked the fire and sent sparks flying.

"I've heard of folks," Barsha went on, "who lived in finer places. One time I saw a picture of the homeplace where the President of Washington lives. A choice picture it made, but it would be a cold and naked place to live in, from the looks. I used to study a heap on different kinds of houses, more especially since Waits come back with news of city places. Makes a person restless."

Fayre nodded a "Yes," and she went on: "Then I got my head contented that it was the folks in 'em that counted. A homeplace takes its set from its folks."

"Not efn its froze," Fayre said, thinking of the bleakness at Ansen's.

"You'll likely keep a fire, I hope," Barsha said sharply. And she got up. "I aim to take a chance on them beans," she said, and walked into the kitchen.

FAYRE spent the night at Lowe's and set forth next morning well thawed out. Waits went along so far as his path led, and Barsha also in the strange bonnet, for she was bent to go so far as Homer Howard's, and not to be denied.

First she craved to visit with Matt Ewart, and Fayre made a long road out of his way to see her so far as the gate. When Matt came to the door she bid him enter with Barsha.

"Get on now," Barsha told him, "get you to work and earn money."

For half an hour the two old women sat by the stove and thought together.

Then Barsha drew a long breath. "They're bent on it," she said. "No power on earth can argue with young folks. The thing I been stubbing my mind on is—what's to do with Homer?"

"What's to hinder him living with them?"

Barsha took off her bonnet and smoothed its ribbons. She looked at Aunt Matt; and time ticked gently in the quiet kitchen.

"That's so," Aunt Matt went on directly, "Bess being the very model of Homer, he'd be a care to her and a misery to himself. Dena and him might get on. O' course," she hurried her words, "I'm knowen how you fail of the space up to your house."

Barsha sat still a long while. The clock whirred eleven strokes; and Matt got up to fetch a pan of potatoes and sat down again to pare them.

"I fail of figuring just how me and Sam could keep him," she said, "Sam being the moving kind."

Barsha got up to go.

"You'll stay eat dinner with us?" Matt asked.

"Kind thanks," Barsha said, "but not this day. I took it in head to eat up at Homer's. Likely they'll have bait of beans or whatever. Bess is a heap better than she was to keep house."

"I've not been up to a meal since long days," Matt owned. "Last time I tramped on Bess's temper, telling her how the saucepans wasn't what they used to be in Dena's time. I'm old enough for better sense, mercy knows! The insides was right enough, but the outsides—and where the handles join on—they garred my fingers twitch."

Barsha stood by the door all this time, and now she stepped down the yard.

"O' course," she said, "it ain't the handiest place in the world for Sam's mill, but it's a choice homestead. Wish you good-day. Come over to ours before long."

Half way up the path to Homer Howard's place, Barsha sat on a handy boulder to draw breath. "Been ages of time since I seen town from this side," she said. "Path like this recalls a person's years."

When she got up so far as the porch, she called her name, and Homer, not believing his ears, failed to bid her enter, but sent Bess to see who was.

Barsha said: "You got no cause to take a spasm, me coming in at dinner time. Half a smidgen of whatever you got will do me."

And being bid, she entered, and sat in talk with Homer, while Bess took the spasm just the same and the house was filled with clatter of things dropped in haste.

In proper time they sat down to the meal and it was worthy of the sudden guest, though the table looked surprised at itself, and Bess was something tousled and hot. Barsha gave praise by eating a piece of every food spread forth, and she told Homer that there were men she'd heard of that failed of being knowen a good housekeeping woman when they had one. After the meal she helped Bess put away, while she and Bess talked about the price of curtains and how much a store-boughten grass rug might cost.

Directly Barsha said: "Happen I might spare a hour or so with Homer, gin you crave a visit with Dena. She's lonely for you these times."

"She never owned as much!" Bess wondered.

"She's got better manners," Barsha said, "and she'd not be complaining how only an old woman days long gets her fretted. You brisk up there and see efn she's content."

When they were alone, Barsha began on Homer. He was a helpless old man, but this was the last thing Barsha wanted him to recall.

"You was always a neighborly one to do a kindness," she began.

Homer perked up. Mostly his neighbors craved to help him, and this had long been his weariness. The last weeks especially he'd been made to feel like a log on every foot.

"Aim to," he said, "but there's poor chance."

"Hit all comes to what you call a poor chance," Barsha said. "There's Sam Ewart now. He can't abide living in a house where a person's died. And Matt's getting so she dreads a new place. Seems like there's no place to go around Glen Hazard. They been in most homesteads, turn about; and Matt's point-blank set against moving to Sunview."

Homer treddaned on this and felt it over and over in his mind, while Barsha stayed quiet and wished she'd had sense to bring along the rug she was hooking.

Then Homer had a notion.

"What's to hinder 'em sharing this place, gin Bess takes Fayre Jones?"

"Homer Howard," Barsha said admiringly, "I never rightly give you credit for the mind you got, nor the heart either. How come you to think o' that!"

"My mind works, odd days," Homer said, while he clicked back and forth in his rocker and contented himself with the sound.

And then there was only common talk of lost days in the backward years; and Homer saying how it was a fortunate thing he had no orchard trees to trouble with, seeing the surprising weather would have started the rot. And Barsha holding on to her manners the way she'd not bid Homer cease that crazy to-and-fro in his own chair and homestead.

Barsha set out the minute she heard Bess coming back, and though night was almost on top of her, she stopped by Sam and Matt Ewart's place on the way home.

Sam was in the yard, wrapped up like a package

for mailing; and having an ax in his hand; and he and the ax looked at the wood for the supper fire.

Barsha seized on the weakness she saw before her. "Gin you was chair-bound, liken to Homer Howard," she said, "you'd no more need to cut wood. He buys his ready cut."

"Come in and eat supper!"

"Not this night; I give promise I'd be home. Happen you've planned ary place to move yet?"

"Who talks of me and moving?" Sam said, as he rolled along to the fence.

"I just allowed you would—after Morris was by."

Matt looked out of the door for the supper wood. "Enter, Barsha!" she called out. "You'll freeze up!"

"I'm going on, I thank you," Barsha said. Her nose was blue and she'd lost all feeling in her hands and feet, but her mind yet spun around and she had no notion of getting in where she might not handily get out without wasted talk.

"Already I used up time at Homer's," she said. "That's the choicest homestead. Once there and a person might be anchored and free of moving."

Matt went in.

"Efn it wasn't useless for a mill site," Sam said,

when he had thought heavily, "I'd favor that place my ownself."

"I'd reckon," Barsha said, " 'twould be handier to move a mill here and there and have a fast homeplace separate. A man's bound to grow a house around him in his last years; but he might shove a mill all over the country. Wish you good-night!"

And she made her way home in the cold darkness and kept her bed three days thereafter with what she called tuckered-outness.

CHAPTER XXVI

OUT of the house at Ansen's Place came a great dust, and there was hammering down at the barn. The yard was newly scraped of trash; and the chickens that Dena and Waits had sent for a present were spread abroad in the low field. Already the place looked lived-in again, for Bess and Fayre Jones were on their homeplace.

There was a big fire in the cookstove and a fierce blaze in the open hearth, so that Fayre coming in hot enough already from his work peeled off his coat in haste and Bess laughed at him, while she set a pot of coffee on an up-turned box, with bread and preserves and a platter of eggs and meat. They sat down among their scattered goods and ate a first meal in their own home; and Bess let her eyes roam eagerly over the furnishments that were standing crazily in wrong corners. She was in such haste to get at things that she jumped up in the midst of each bite to tug at the sofa, or to try a picture against the wall.

"Set down," Fayre said, "and leave a man eat!"

"Which corner," Bess said seriously, "do you reckon the bed'll be warmest?"

"Hit ain't even a bed yet, Mis' Bearm. The head 'n' foot's yet on the porch and the rails is back o' the stove."

"Never did I feel more content," Bess said, while she carried a heap of used dishes to a corner shelf that was already full. "Time you fetch me a pail o' water I'll do the dishes, and you can hurry so's to be ready and help me twitch things in place gin it comes dark. Where at's the candles, now I think? I hope we get to fetch a table afore the week's out. Tables is the handiest thing. Fayre Jones, you failed of bringing that box from home—the one that says SOUP on it—hit's got candles and the lamp in. What'll we do?"

"First place," Fayre told her, "you hush talking so's my mind can hear itself work."

He stretched himself tall by the stove, and being that way up he plucked an old fly-paper off the ceiling and burned it.

"Screens," he said thoughtfully, "and a wire door. Who's that hollering?"

Bess ran to the window.

"Hit's Micajah," she said, making a twisted face, "that old buzzard's got no call to croak at our door."

Fayre was so content, being warm and fed and home, that he was pleasured to see even this company. He stepped to the door, stealing a kiss of his wife's back neck as he went.

Bess heard him call: "Hi, 'Cajah!"

And Micajah said: "Come out here, I got a piece o' business."

She ran to the window and pressed against it, her heart suddenly tight. She tried to hear what the talk was, but the two were leaning on the gate far out of ears' length. And Fayre was wilting already, and his face gone blank and fearful. What did that devil of a slackentwist say? Bess held on to the window ledge and felt bad news trickling all over her. "Fayre promised he'd not have more dealings with him," she said aloud. "He give me his harsh promise not to!" Yet Fayre was so limp and willing did any person ask a favor.

Bess dragged herself from the window and stirred fretfully about the room, shifting things around and doing no good. But she kept coming back to peer out. Micajah was gone away now, and Fayre came up the path with all the joy gone out of him, and he came in and slumped on a box by the stove. Bess waited. And the things standing around were only a mess and a weariness and no more the makings of a home.

"I might have been knowen," Fayre said, "ary thing I aim for goes agley."

"Ne'er a thing can touch us, not so's to hurt. We got us a homeplace!"

Fayre got up and paced the floor. "That's what we ain't got," he wailed. "Me thinking all was done and over. This place ain't any more ours than—than nothing." He turned on Bess. "What ailed you to wed with a lackbrain?" he quarreled. "You were knowen I'd not got any up-'n'-at-it. All town's 'ware of that, and never fails of saying it. I'm a jolterhead, I'm a flinch, I'm a noggen."

"No help now," Bess said, "since Virge Howard fast wed us and Ranson Gillow witnessed. Happen you come out with the tale, I'll likely catch up on what you say."

"Seems Micajah has got him a mortgage over this place and it past due."

Misery was in every corner of the house. It was scarce worthwhile fixing up things when they'd be moving out directly. An hour gone, such things as cracked window-panes and loose ceiling boards were matters to be planned about. Now they were just more things gone to wrack.

Bess had the scowl of one who thinks all around a thing and gets no further.

"Surely that's Ansen's affairs. 'Twould be in his name."

"He failed of naming in the trade that his title wasn't cleared," Fayre said.

Later he went on. " 'Course—I might work it out."

"You give harsh promise not."

"Believe I'll go talk with Waits Lowe and chance his calling me a trusting innocent."

"And leave me in this darkling house with all things standing on one leg?" Bess said. "Tell you what I believe—I believe you'll go up home and get that box with the lamp in. Time you're back I'll have the place froshed up fit so's to live."

She turned from him and leaned her hot forehead against a chilling window-pane, and the frozen yard glittered and danced beyond her tears, and she had to wait to make her voice firm. And so Fayre should not guess she was crying, she spoke fiercely: "We got this place, and we keep it," she said. "We keep it gin the devil's ownself!"

Fayre wrapped his coat around him and pulled his cap down over his eyes and set forth. She called after him: "Hasten and be back before nightfall. And never give one word of talk to whosoever—not to whosoever. And watch you'll keep a shut mouth to Homer. Him and Sam and Aunt Matt's only just getting suited. Come you unsettle 'em 'twould be a mix."

IN the middle of that night, Fayre sat up in bed.

" 'Twould take more money to prove by law that Ansen ought to pay mortgage than 'twould to pay it."

"Mercy's patience, Fayre Jones, d'you yet fail of sleep. Likely the roof'll stay on till morning's light!"

They both lay wakeful.

"Fayre!"

"Yes, Little Thing?"

"Place'll be a picture gin that runner rose covers the front fence line."

"How long?"

"I got a sight many slips. Be about a year beyond June."

"Fayre!"

"?"

" 'Twill look a picture?"

"Yes, Little Thing."

THE roof stayed on all night and the best of the following week; but there was not so much heart in homemaking with the place shaking under them; and a mort of things were left standing unwrapped in case happen . . .

And when Ed Gillow made his way up a soon day thereafter, he found Bess hanging curtains as if decking the house for a funeral.

"Fayre'll be home any next minute," she said, when she had bid him to a chair. "He'll be proud efn you'll stay and eat."

Ed plucked up his cap. "Kind of soon days to be visiting with fresh married folks," he excused himself, "but I've not got only two-three days home."

"We're not fixed up to treat you clever, but you're rightly welcome to what we got. And we ain't fresh married. I mean to say it might be a year or more."

Ed thought most likely a quarrel so soon, and when Fayre came in looking solemn as a gravestone, Ed wished he'd been quick-minded and gone on home. But he had already consented, and they got through supper without any up-fuss.

And afterwards Bess said: "Ed's been to school —likely he'll be knowen."

Fayre said: "I never heard of school doing a man's mind much good—excusing Ed, o' course."

"Reckon I'll be going on," Ed said, greatly afraid of being invited into trouble.

"Set still," Fayre ordered him, "and hear the history."

Ed kept pace with Fayre's story by nodding and shaking his head and saying: "Shucks!" and "That so?" And when all was told he stayed a long time in thought.

"I got a notion . . ." he began. "Reckon I'll be going on," he ended. " 'Night to you all."

When Ed was gone off, Fayre stirred the fire and pulled off his shoes the better to toast his feet.

"Perfectly like I 'wared you," he told Bess, "that's schooling. You 'n' me is knowen of that much, and come by it cheaper."

CHAPTER XXVII

FROM the stir in Glen Hazard it might have been Election Day. The slow sun put no heart into his work and all town was shivering. The citizens stood around with coats buttoned close, and caps pulled down on their ears so they said: "What?" and "Disabled to tell what you say!" when they spoke together. And they stamped to keep their feet warm.

The news of Fayre Jones' mischance had gone abroad, and betwixt Fayre and Micajah there was no doubt which side Glen Hazard favored. Micajah might be a sneaking go-by-ground and Fayre might be overly trusting, but do as they would in recalling all the bright side of Fayre it did seem that 'Cajah had the rights of the law.

Better news also came out, how the officers were hunting Micajah for the road damage. And they named Dite Morgan a sneap, the way he'd laid out on a man he had worked like partners with and gone off and taken up with the railroad.

Now Fayre and Micajah during this time were

in back of Ranson Gillow's store along with Ranson himself, and Sheriff Joe Marks, and Ed Gillow, whose notion was now full grown and about to bear fruit.

"I'll have the money or the place," Micajah said, "and I'll not complain which."

The Sheriff said to Fayre: "You'd ought to have studied on this afore ever you traded. Which'll you do? 'Cajah's got the rights."

"Carry three," Ranson Gillow said, from where he was doing figures at the end of the table, "which'll be three hundred, near as I can come it."

Fayre Jones chafed up and down the room and carefully pushed back a tack that was leaving the county road map fly off the wall. Directly he said: "Neither! 'Cajah ain't done right. He'd ought to have 'wared me."

"Three hundred and some odds over," Ranson Gillow said.

Sheriff Marks reasoned with Fayre: "Hit's Nels Ansen should have 'wared you; and for the matter of that it was you should have found out was the title fitten for trading. You been neglectful."

Micajah writhed himself around a chair back, and said: "I give him three chances—cash money, work it out, or I take the place. I'll not say more. A man's got to live."

"A pity," Marks said.

The door opened, due to Uncle Shannon Budd's eagerness getting the better of his manners, and when Ed Gillow had slammed it shut again, they could hear the old man shouting to all without: "They ain't moving none—jes' setting, that's all."

Ranson Gillow folded up his papers that he'd been figuring and handed them to the Sheriff. He had a kindness to offer, and failing of how to come at it, he said to Marks: "You edzact it out, Joe; I got to go tend store."

Micajah cried out: "Stay set! We got to have witnesses, and the more the sounder."

Ranson was pointedly out of patience with him. "No person ever heard tell of Fayre Jones breaking his harsh promise yet."

"Happen 'Cajah craves witnesses," Marks said, "we're all here. And here's the store bill for 'Cajah's three years' back credit that Ranson's handed to me to collect."

"Eh?" Micajah said.

"Three seasons you been overdue," Marks told him, "and you may as well own it now as then."

"Hell's Banjer! I give you a note for it," Micajah snapped.

"And failed of paying it," Marks finished for him. "I got that note. Gin it gets paid, you'll maybe get a receipted bill."

"Ranson Gillow!" Micajah shouted, "efn you ain't the downgonest! You owe me for . . ." But he saw the Sheriff's eyes on him and ended sorrowfully: "I'm a poor man."

"So's Fayre Jones a poor man."

"Adding us together don't make either of us rich," Micajah quarreled. "A eye for a tooth is what the Bible says."

"None said you'd not get it," the Sheriff said mildly. "Now, Fayre Jones, listen here!"

Fayre stood still.

"Ed Gillow had a notion . . ."

"I'm bound to get on No. 6," Ed broke in. "Wish you good-day!" and he went off in a swivvet.

"And he talked about it with Ranson . . ."

"That mail will be here in half a switch," Ranson said, and went out.

Sheriff Marks plodded on: "You recall me being tripped up so I failed of bringing in Ed on a liquor charge?"

Fayre nodded.

And Micajah said: "*That's* where it got to!"

"I failed of being knowen who done that," Marks said to Fayre, "till Ed owned it was you. Well, Ranson had no more than paid for Ed's schooling in the city, and gin he failed of going, owing to being in jail, the money'd not have been paid back. And as a consequence, owing to you saving him that loss, Ranson's willing to swap his note on 'Cajah for 'Cajah's mortgage on Ansen's Place."

"Perfectly obliged to him," Fayre said, all in a mix, "but it yet fails of being clear just where that'll mend things."

Micajah saw what was fast enough, and he howled: "I'll not do it—'tain't sound law!"

Marks shut him up and worked it out: "Micajah gets back his store note; and you, Fayre Jones, owe the mortgage to Ranson Gillow, and can pay it at ease and not be turned adrift."

"And I lose . . ." Micajah started.

"Ne'er a one of the three loses a thing," Marks said, "only Micajah Dobbs pays his rightful debts by a accident."

Fayre drew a long breath and got his life right side up again.

"You're point-blank certain," he asked, "that Ranson'll not lose a thing?"

"Ranson's got a heap better chance of getting the mortgage out of you than of getting cash money by 'Cajah; and I'd not be surprised but you're best content to work out your homeplace than just to heir to it free."

No. 6 having run by this time along, the Sheriff and Fayre went out and mingled with the townsmen, while Micajah took out the back way and was lost from sight.

"Looks to me," Fayre said slowly to Marks, "that Nels Ansen come off proudest out of this deal."

A hantle of road officers had come up from the city on No. 6 and they now called for Micajah at Marks' hands that he should deliver him unto them, for they had learned from the townsmen how a man of that name was hid in the back room of the store. And Marks said: "Skin your own skunks."

So one of the officers set forth to search the town, and weaved his way among the citizens asking first of one and then of another: "Can any of you men tell me where I'll find a man called Dobbs —Micajah Dobbs?"

"What like is he?" each asked carefully.

"Tall fellow, yellow hair, blue eyes. I got a warrant to bring him up over this road accident last fall."

"Been long along," Newt Beechy said. "Maybe he died in the plague these forerunning weeks."

And the man asked again, and the more he asked the more there wasn't any answer until he was altogether misput and out of patience, and Newt Beechy took pity on him.

"Micajah Dobbs?" Newt puzzled, "tall man, you say? and yellow-haired? Leave me study a while."

The roadman waited, and in due time Newt said: "We ain't got any tall yellow men called Dobbs in theseabouts. Why not you try over to Robbins' Gap—they keep a slew o' queer folk over yon ways."

CHAPTER XXVIII

WAIT-STILL-ON-THE-LORD LOWE came forth from his cabin with a light tread. Not since the days of his setting out to see the world had he tingled so keenly with the joy of living.

"Hi-yar!" he cried out, while he stamped his feet in the crisp snow. "This morning's air is eager!"

And he pranced along the new road until he came to the righthand opportunity that leads down to Ansen's Place, and here, for all his haste to get down to Fayre and Bess and tell them his news, he stopped to look at the good world.

The woods were magic white in the still and piercing cold. Every tree bole was sheathed in ice and each branch and twig of the forest covered an inch thick in it. Through the tender gray of the sky a brightness from the thin-veiled sun caught and flashed upon the silver net of the woods, and the topmost branches of the tall trees reached like cables high into the heavens. A tinkling like broken glass sounded from afar off as some young tree snapped and shattered from its too great load. Silver light lay in the hollows and the air smelled clean.

"The whole earth's bound to the feet of the Lord with cords of silver," Waits chanted as he stood and breathed deeply of the wholesome air. It tasted crisp and went straight to his head, sending him forward at a run; and as he went he sang: "Skip-to-ma'-Lou—hi-yaddy-ee-ee!—'or ever the silver cord be snapped or the golden bowl be broken'—Lord Almighty, how the Bible words lend sense to the world! The silver cord can't be a thing else but a youngling in a great snûd to be otherwhere. And talking of younglings—— Mankind! but it's the spryest day!"

When he came to Ansen's Place, he cried the house so loud that Fayre and Bess both came running to see what damage might be happening.

They called him to enter, but he was far past roofs this day, and marched up and down in the snow, laughing aloud one minute and scowling himself sober the next.

"Come out with the news," Fayre said. "*You* may likely be outgate the senses, but *I'm* not; and it's a cold day. Either come in house or leave me go back by the fire."

" 'Tain't nothing uncommon," Waits said at last, trying to make his voice sound ordinary, "not a thing out o' the way." And he cut a double shuffle that sent a cloud of snow all over him.

"Great forever, Waits Lowe," Bess said, "be at it! I'm about to freeze stiff."

So Waits told them his news. And it was the commonest thing on earth, only next early summer Dena promised him a child-thing, and this happening, taken together with a fresh day, had set him off with a queerness, and seeing it would get bettermost of him he craved to tell it out, and here he was.

Fayre watched him seriously. Likely it would take Waits just this way. He hoped himself would have more soberness when his turn came.

"Well," he said at last, "I'm proud for you, surely—but what else did you look for?"

Bess being in a great taking about going to see Dena right away, Fayre owned he'd as well spend the day idling along with Waits, and they got into their coats and high shoes and came out to him.

There were silver flowers of frost in handy corners, and the lone bird they saw from the gate of their homestead was high and far with distance in its wings.

And the three went together cheerfully through the snow.

They came to the top of Cragg Hill and crossed at a long slant.

"Yon runs a rabbit!" Waits cried out. "Look at him jump!"

"This old road'll be fading out o' memory," Fayre said. "Come fall of the year drifted leaves'll be settled in the rain gullies."

"Roads come 'n' go," Waits said. "The wide open road will go through, yet its time'll come. We go down the silver road today and we'll see days together—hours in hid hollows, years of hours filled with living, time that's bright and smooth beyond all saying."

"We're out o' the way o' roads," Bess said. "You down your side and us on ours. Leave the old road fade. There's roads, and folks, and things happening. . . ." She trailed off, disabled to keep her mind on what she tried to say.

"You fail of being knowen the meaning of the words you say," Waits plagued her.

"You likewise," Bess said. "You say 'yon runs a rabbit.' What's a rabbit? Answer me that and you dare, Waits Lowe! Gin you named it a squirrel 'twould hop just as quick."

Waits thought about this while he got over the fence and Fayre picked up Bess and handed her over to him.

They went down the sharp slant toward Lowe's and yet he could not say what a rabbit might be. Always such times as he craved to be upsides of Bess she had a thing he failed of being knowen.

Barsha was ready for them, and mainly proud to be doing around the house again, the way she cosseted Dena and kept the menfolk under sharp orders. And the curved shadows on her face were grown deeper than in former times.

A wholesome day they spent, and ended it around a pine-log fire. And in the firelight with their shadows spread against the dark log walls till all the world was only the warm circle of brightness, they were one clan—Waits and Dena on the fire's far side, content yet fearful in their waiting; Fayre and Bess on the hither side, thinking it almost time to be going home and full of mischief at the notion; Rashe and Barsha before the fire, watching it flicker and fade the way they had seen so many fires die down on that same hearth.

Rashe stirred from his chair and got his Bible off the corner shelf and sought among its leaves a long while for a chapter to content him, while his eyes screwed up to make out the small print in the flickering light. Waits kicked the fire brighter and threw on a pine knot; and by its hearty blaze, Rashe made out the story of Jacob serving for Rachel; and his voice was rich in the quiet room.

"So it all come right after long years," he said, "saving for the mischance of getting Leah first; and I reckon she had her uses like most drawbacks."

He closed the book and laid it on his knee.

"What do folk get out of loving and wedding at long last?" Fayre asked, folding Bess's hand in his.

"Young-uns," Waits said readily, "and the world starting again as a consequence."

"A homeplace," Bess said, "and each other to care for, and—just a heap o' things that fail of rightly going in words. You say what 'tis, Mis' Lowe."

"Rashe will tell you, I reckon," Barsha answered.

"I been wise enough a'ready," Rashe said. "Hit's with us the way it was with Jacob—joy and hardness mixed 'twel a person fails of recalling it all."

They went back to their own quietness till long along, and the fire shrank up to a glow.

And at last Barsha said: "And all we get when all's done is a homesome voice to speak to us at the day's end; and a hand to touch in a darkened room. Give us that, and we fail of caring what has gone. Give us that and what's to come holds no threat."

FAYRE and Bess came home in the cold evening through the swift quietness of the snow.

And when they were above their homeplace, they stopped and looked down to where it lay sleeping in the shadows. They stood as if they might have been strangers, fearful to break the ghostly stillness.

"Might not be ours yet," Bess said, " 'tis more a dream place, from the looks. The moon and snow steal it now."

Bess drew near to Fayre and he put an arm around her.

" 'Tis ours to keep," he said. "Long years of days will come to us."

"I'm pointedly scared to go down."

"We'll rattle the door to give whatever ghosts

are there a chance to run ere we enter," Fayre laughed at her.

But she was very serious when she said: "And we'll leave the door stand wide till we get the lamp safe lit."

And they went down into the quiet hollow where their homeplace lay.

THE END

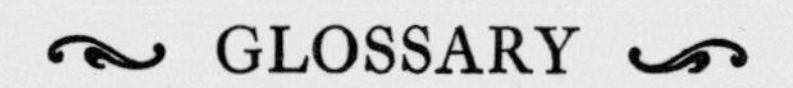

GLOSSARY

GLOSSARY

BANTLING–cradle-child, baby.

BEARM–emotion, stir, excitement.

BOBBLE–a clumsy mistake, fumble, "to make a mess of."

BODACIOUSLY–altogether, out-and-out.

BRABBLE–confusion, SPRATTLE.

CADDLE–mix-up, disorder.

CHIP–graft, bud; but also CHIP OUT–to fall out, have a misunderstanding.

COOTER–spud around, mose, brogue, etc.

COSSET–pet, cuddle, fondle.

CÛD–friendly, kind, affable.

CUMFLUTTERED–all put about by excitement.

DONEY GAL–sweetheart.

DOUT–do out; like "doff" from "do off."

DUMMOCK–stupid one, thick head.

EMBRANGLED–entangled, confused.

FECKLESS–useless, helpless (Old Scotch).

FERE–brotherly, companionable, sympathetic.

FLINCH–coward.

FORENENST–against.

FOSSICKING–rummaging, restlessing.

FOZY–lacking substance, wandering in mind, not overly bright.

FRECKET–peevish.

FROGGING–"how you frogging?"—how you getting along; how are you?

FROSH–furbished up, polished.

GAR–to force or compel.

GIRT–diagonally; "to go

girt" is to cross at a slant.

GLIB–free, slippy, smooth.

GLIRRED–glided and slid.

GRAMY–to vex; also "mixed up," "put out," "made miserable."

HANTLE–a small gathering or crowd; as distinct from KENNING and SKAIL, which see.

HARDNESS–ill-will.

HIRPLE–hasten awkwardly.

JOLTER-HEAD–simpleton.

JOWER–serious quarrel; ripe anger.

KENNING–large crowd.

KURLING–hastening, hurrying, getting along with speed.

LOSEL–good-for-nothing, wastrel.

LOWN–mild, soft.

MASTER–(*adv.*) very much, exceedingly; i. e. in masterly style.

MELL–mix, mill, stir.

MIRK–murky, dark.

MONGLE–botch, awkwardness.

MORNGLÔM–the morning twilight, an hour before full dawn.

MORT–a great deal, a lot of.

MUCKER–(1) damage or mess, see also CADDLE; (2) envious, covetous.

MULL-HEADED–headachy with fever.

MULLOCK–mess of disorder, an upheaval.

MUZZY–muddled in the wits.

NIDGET–scary one, "jump-shadow."

NOGGEN–clumsy; goose!

ONDING–a pelting downpour of rain.

OVERBRAEDEN–spread over, overcast, cover with.

PATHERY–nervous, fretful, fidgety.

RAPPED–traded, swapped.

RIPPIT–fist-fight.

RUCTION–quarrel.

SCAWTING–boasting, bragging.

SCUNNERED–badly frightened, terrified.

SHOG–take one's self off, get along.

SHUMMICK–shuffle, to drag the feet, fret to and fro, idle along.

SIB–kin to; "one of us."

SKAIL–a crowd of people in motion.

SLACKENTWIST–trifler, dawdler; i.e. SLACK-TWISTED.

SLIMPSEY–poor quality, shoddy material.

SLOM–completely, all the way; "kettle turned slom over," i. e. upside down.

SMIDGEN–small portion, little bit.

SMOOCH–sulk.

SNEAPING–sneaking or spying.

SNIRLY–rough.

SNÛD–a hurry, a rush.

SPRATTLE–fuss, a falling out, noisy words.

SPUD–to amble around, to loiter.

STIVING–lazy.

SURVIGROUS–great, excessive; term of superlative degree.

SWITCH–moment, instant, "this minute."

SWIVVET–an anxious rush, haste.

TRAG–evil, mean, bad (not used of persons).

TREDDAN–to think upon, to study over, turn over in the mind.

TRIVVET–wild one, flyabout.

TUTLY–captious, irritable, "touchy."

UPSCUDDLE–a bitter, fighting quarrel.

WEIGHT–blame, responsibility.

WIDDING–idling.

WISTLY–eager, alert.

WORD-OF-A-SORT–"a piece of my mind."